# THE ENEMY NEXT DOOR

# THE ENEMY NEXT DOOR

REBEL HART

# 1

## TATIANA

I picked out the nicest dress I had in my closet that wouldn't make it look like I was headed to a wedding or a funeral. A lime-green halter dress with pink strawberries on it seemed as good a choice as any. When paired with a cream cardigan, my favorite pair of roman sandals, and my golden brown, wavy hair hanging freely at my shoulders, I felt good that I was dressed impressively enough. I was dancing around my room to the music of my heart racing wildly, barely able to contain my excitement to head to school for the day. Even just having to come home and go to sleep seemed to be too long; I wanted to get back to Colin.

He finally kissed me.

I walked over to my dresser and picked up the

newest addition to my jewelry collection, a thin, gold chain, on the end of which half of a small, football shaped locket hung. Colin had the other half. I'd saved for close to a year in order to buy it. The day I saw it in the window of the kitschy sports shop at the mall, was the same day I realized I'd fallen in love with Colin Undinger. His parents had taken us with them to do some school shopping at the mall and after grabbing my hand to pull me out of the way of some oncoming moms with strollers, he decided to continue to hang on after the danger had passed. Our parents were high school friends, so we'd known one another our entire lives, but that was the first time I started to see him as more than just my best friend.

We were still so young, but even as a spritely seventh grader, I knew that I wanted him to kiss me. I wanted him to be my first kiss and my second and my third. I thought that he liked me back when he held my hand, but he never did anything else and I was too afraid of rejection to venture to find out. I settled for continued friendship until the day I bought a football locket for us each to take a half of, inspiring him to finally kiss me during sunset in front of the same mall. I couldn't keep myself from foolishly thinking we were going to eventually get married at that mall; it had been such a staple land-mark in the development of our relationship.

A kiss was more telling than a hand hold, but I still didn't ask Colin how he really felt about me just yet. I wanted to dress my best, sit him down, and ask him properly; today was that day.

I skipped downstairs with my locket in hand, and walked into the kitchen. My parents were standing around the kitchen island, sipping coffee, and nibbling on bacon. I hopped up on one of the island chairs and held the locket out to my mom to help me put on. Both she and my dad were eyeing me through peaked eyebrows and suspicious smirks.

"What?" I asked.

My mom walked over and took the necklace from me, holding it up and letting it dangle in the sun streaming in from the window. "This is nice. I didn't know *you* were into football." She said it in a way that let me know she already knew the answer to her inquiry.

I smiled as she laced it around my neck and clasped it. I touched it gently where the locket hung at my collarbone. "I bought it for Colin and me."

My dad tilted his head, his curly black mop top and salt and pepper goatee making his piqued interest more whimsical. "It looks nice. How did you afford it?"

"I saved up my allowance for a year." Pride filled my body. It felt so good having my hard work for a year lead to my first kiss with my first love.

"Wow." My mom set a plate with some bacon and eggs and a cup of orange juice down in front of me. "It must have been important to you." She sideyed my dad and they shared a knowing glance. "What did Colin do?"

I remembered the feeling of his soft lips on mine. I'd heard horror stories about awkward first kisses. Neither person knows what to do and it's quick and sloppy and unexpected. I'd always told myself that it didn't matter how the kiss went, as long as it happened; a kiss with someone you loved was good regardless. When I noticed Colin leaning in, I started to prepare myself mentally. I knew it was going to be awkward. But his lips brushed gently against mine in a barely there peck before settling into place and drawing my very breath from my mouth. I sunk against him naturally, trying to emblazon it into my mind. When we parted, an eternity had passed, but it had still been too short, all I wanted was to do it again.

"He was happy." I realized too much time had passed since I responded and the silence answered for me.

My mom kissed me on the top of my head. "I'm glad."

"Me too." My dad finished his coffee and set his mug in the sink. "I think I'll have to talk to Colin soon."

I didn't realize what he meant at the time, but I didn't care. All that mattered to me was getting to Colin again and chasing a second kiss.

I finished my breakfast and, after saying goodbye to my mom, went to my dad's he-should-have-retired-it-years-ago, navy blue Corolla. My school was only about two blocks from my house, but my dad worked at the school district office right across the street, so he drove me because it was faster. We lived in a small, everyone knows everyone town outside of Grand Junction, Colorado called Orchard Mesa with a population of less than 10,000 people. All of the students in Orchard Mesa went to one of the three schools we had, either the elementary school, the middle school, or the high school and they were all located in the 'Quad' a spit of land where the district office and all three schools all sat kitty corner from one another. Colin and I were in middle school, but we'd known one another for as long as either of us could remember.

My dad pulled up in front of the school and I was a little disappointed to see that Colin wasn't standing there waiting for me like normal. I knew that the results of last week's football tryouts were going to be posted, but I thought he would still wait. He'd always been a fan of football and I didn't have any doubt in my mind that he'd make the A team. Only the high school had a varsity and junior varsity team, while the middle school didn't turn any students down, per se, but they were divided into A, B, and C teams based on their skill level. There were no other schools to play against in Orchard Mesa, so the tiered teams helped the school determine who their opponents would be. Colin had been playing football on rec teams since he was old enough to do so, and had waited excitedly for the day he could try out for the first Orchard Mesa team he could, Middle School A. I celebrated the occasion with the football locket I'd bought him, the one he'd immediately dubbed his good luck charm.

I didn't need to see him to know that he'd made the A team, but that didn't stop me from hopping out of my dad's car without even saying goodbye and heading into the school with a little pep in my step. Those who tried to greet me on the way in got little response, I had the love of my life to get to--to congratulate him on his latest achievements. I imagined myself sitting on the bleachers on a chilly fall night, wrapped in one of Colin's jackets, cheering him on during one of his games. The very thought made every part of me tingle with warmth and excitement.

It was going to be a good year.

The entrance of the school was packed with all of the middle school's students in a concentrated area. I didn't realize that the sports tryouts results would be posted right inside the front door. What teachers had hoped would be a quick glance and pass for the students had turned into a blood clot. I stood on my tippy toes, peering over the crowd in search of the one I wanted to see. He was taller than most kids our age, so I knew he'd be easy to identify.

My heart did a backflip. Over the tops of the sea of students, was the top of Colin's head. His long brown hair was pulled back behind his head in a messy bun. The sun shone from his face with his emerald eyes shining and a smile sliding from ear to ear. It was as much as a confirmation as I needed: he definitely made the team. If that wasn't enough of an indicator, the dozens of other students clamoring to talk to him certainly was.

I pushed my way through the crowd. Insults and swear words were raining down on me for my apparent gall for just trying to get to my...

boyfriend? Could I say that already? No. I should definitely wait until we had talked about it.

I'd made it to about three rows back before the wall of students was clasped so tightly I had no hope of getting any closer. As annoying as I found it, I had no choice but to wait until Colin noticed me or the teachers broke up the pack and I could get to him easier.

"I knew you'd make it, Colin," one girl with a blond bob cut sang to him. "I saw your tryout."

"Oh, really?" Colin's voice was sweet and inviting. "That's so nice of you that you came."

"Of course I came. I wanted to support you." She combed her hand through her hair. "Actually, I was hoping that maybe you'd want to go out with me sometime?"

The girl next to her started giggling. "She's liked you for a long time."

"Really?" Colin's left hand went to his right arm to massage his bicep. "That's cool. Sure, we can do that."

It was so shocking I felt like I was going to awaken from a nightmare at any second. I looked around at the students standing next to me, as if maybe one of them would have heard what I heard, and magically know why I found that so painful. Colin kissed me, I thought he liked *me*, why would he agree to go out with another girl?

The blond started to squeal. "Really? Okay! Maybe we could go to the Sadie Hawkins dance together?"

The Sadie Hawkins dance was a dance that took place at the night of the first football game every year. Only 7th and 8th graders could go, and it was tradition for the girls to ask the boys to be their dates instead of the other way around. Guys only ever agreed to go with girls they liked, everyone knew that.

Colin laughed. "Maybe!"

My heart broke.

I touched the football locket hanging at my collarbone, praying for it to shoot me back in time. Had I misread something somewhere along the way? Did Colin not actually like me and just do the things that I thought were romantic as a sign of friendship?

I was an idiot.

I turned around and forced my way through the masses until I was back at the front door. I ran outside with tears already cascading down from my cocoa eyes. I wanted to just run home. The amazing day I'd had at the mall, that wonderful kiss, it was all dripping off of me and falling into tearstained puddles on the ground.

"Um, excuse me?" I looked over and one of the girls who'd previously been standing with the blond that Colin talked to. "Are you okay?"

"Yeah," I snipped back, not wanting to get into it, especially with her. "What do you want?"

She seemed taken aback by the harshness of my tone. "Oh, um. No, I just know that you're really good friends with Colin Undinger, right?"

*Yes. Apparently too good.*

"Why?" I circumvented the question I was afraid to answer.

"I've seen you guys together a lot and my friend asked him to the Sadie Hawkins dance and I just wanted to make sure that you didn't already ask him or something. Are you guys boyfriend and girlfriend?"

I didn't know how to respond to that question. I'd believed we would be. When I woke up that morning, all I could think about was making things official and being a real couple. I never could have expected that, when I got to school, I'd find that things hadn't actually meant as much to him as they did to me.

Like a roach, something deep inside me crawled out wanting to defend me from any more pain. If

Colin honestly thought it was okay to kiss me on Saturday and then come to school on Monday and agree to go to the Sadie Hawkins dance with some other girl, what responsibility did I have to sing his praises to someone else.

Screw him.

"Gross." I wiped my eyes of their tears hoping they would take all my feelings for Colin with them. "I would never be his girlfriend."

The girl looked truly shocked. "Is he a player or something?"

Before I got the chance to answer, Colin appeared out of the corner of my eye. He had a frown on his face and a look of bewilderment; guess he didn't realize that I'd overheard him. I stood up from where I'd planted myself and looked right at him.

"Yeah. I wouldn't trust him." I grabbed the football locket and tugged, snapping it from my neck in a single, swift motion. I tossed it to the ground at his feet, turned my back to him and his new girlfriend's inquirer, and left, promising never to let myself be taken advantage of again.

## 2

# TATIANA

I awoke with a start. My knuckles were white from gripping the sheets and my stomach was trying to arrange a game of musical chairs with the rest of my internal organs. It pissed me off. It was just a dream about a boy from five years ago--why did it still affect me like that?

I looked around my room, drenched in muted tones of grays and blacks, entirely different from the flowery, vibrant room of my past. It was safe to say my first heartbreak jaded me--sapped color from my world--not that it mattered much to me. I'd learned an important lesson that day, not to take people at face value. If someone *could* be lying to you, they probably were, and that was that. I'd love to say that a lot of people came along in the last five years to teach me that I could trust and love again, but the truth was, I never let anyone get that close. I didn't want anyone to be. If going through life with someone at my side was going to leave me as crushed as Colin had, I was better off getting through life myself.

"Tati! Are you awake?" A few quiet knocks followed my mom's voice across my closed door. "Do you want some breakfast?"

"No," I responded, sitting up from my bed. "I'm not hungry."

"Sweetie, I really think you should eat breakfast before school. Studies show--"

"I'm not hungry!" I closed my eyes and sighed. I'd raised my voice unexpectedly to my parents more than once. My shitty past experiences weren't their fault; they were good parents. "I'm sorry. I'm just not quite awake yet."

My mom didn't respond right away. "...A banana?"

"Sure, mom." My tone was flat.

Her footsteps were off down the hallway seconds later.

I reached my arms above my head and stretched, The hope was that, if I stretched tall enough, the memories of my dream would just slide off me and slink back to whatever hole they crawled out of. I stood up and began my daily morning shuffle of selecting a sweater from the several I had that all looked like they belonged on the same black color swatch. Like my room, my wardrobe had been drained of its hue in the wake of my heartbreak and had remained dulled ever since. Suddenly wearing bright colors made me think I stood out too much, I just wanted to blend into Colorado's hazy gray sky--to not be seen.

Cell phone, headphones, and book bag collected, I left my room and headed down into the kitchen. I avoided my usual far right barstool; it was the same place I'd sat that morning. With my dream fresh on my mind, I wanted to distance myself from anything even remotely related. My dad was standing at the counter with a pan frying bacon, the smell of which made my stomach growl at me.

I perched my head in my hand. "Is it too late to ask for bacon?"

My dad looked over his shoulder at me. "It's never too late to ask for bacon." He turned his attention back to the pan. "Are you feeling okay this morning?"

My dad was hyper-observant, always had been. He always said that it was because Portuguese men had no choice but to always have their eyes open. I wish he'd taught me that lesson a little sooner. He'd put the skills to good use as a surveyor for the Orchard Mesa Public School district.

"I didn't sleep well," I lied. "I'm okay."

"Well, young women who don't sleep well get extra bacon." He pulled the pieces he'd already been working on from the pan, set them on a napkin, and slid them over to me. "Careful."

I waited a few seconds for a little more of the bacon's grease to soak into the napkin before nibbling. "Thanks."

"Let me just get some more done for your mother, then we'll go." Even as a licensed 17-year-old in the state of Colorado, my dad still insisted on driving me to school.

"I'll be in the car." I swiped up the napkin of bacon and made my way out into the cooling Colorado air.

Fall was well underway in Orchard Mesa, and the tall trees and gulch-esque. shrubs were going from a lush green to an autumn palette of red, orange, and gold. The ones that had already fell from the branches crunched under my feet as I made myself comfortable in the front passenger's seat of my dad's car; the same old Corolla I'd remembered in my dream. At least some things never changed. The door, I left, tipped open with my leg sticking out and stuck my earbuds in.

Time seemed to flow at a different pace when I had my music playing in my ears. One second I was sitting and waiting for my dad to come out, then next I was sitting in the lunchroom at school with four periods already in my rearview mirror. The only thing I ever counted down the minutes to didn't happen until the second half of my day, so I didn't pay much attention to the first half. I'd hide an earbud behind my back-length tresses, and treat my teachers like all the adults from a Charlie Brown cartoon. Most of the school work was so easy for me that I could do it without the aid of an instructor anyway, and even if it wasn't, I still probably wouldn't care.

I sat at a table in the corner alone until I was finally joined by my only friend to speak of, Billy Bento, aka Wet Willy Billy, the school freak who made the egregious mistake of peeing his pants during a school play in the sixth grade. There wasn't much wrong with him, not like a movie where the school rejects were covered in pimples and taped together glasses. Billy had a regular head of blond hair, gelled and styled to stand up slightly before swooping off to the right. He had a blemish free face and was an average weight and height for his age. His voice wasn't overly nasally, though he did have braces. I guess in Orchard Mesa if you tick just one of the boxes, you might as well tick all of them? Between his wire-covered teeth and tragic backstory, he was Orchard Mesa's mocked mascot.

He sat down next to me. "Hey, Tati."

I finally pulled out my earbuds for the first time since I put them in that morning. "Hey."

"Are you busy after school today? I wanted to try and get our History project charted out." He was already pulling the textbook out of his bag, ignoring his nutritious plate of macaroni or maybe corn. "I was thinking we could do a flip book and while I'm flipping it you could do a speed read like warnings at the end of a commercial. It'd be funny and we'd be done in like two minutes."

"Can we do it tomorrow? I have physics after school today." I said it halfheartedly even though we both knew it was heavier than what it sounded like.

"You're still… tutoring?" Billy's blue eyes had deep concern seated just behind them.

I shrugged. "I need it."

Billy shook his head. "No, you don't."

"Yeah, I do." I fanned around the lunchroom. "One of them is going to *tutor* me?"

He looked around. "I mean… I've heard some of them are good… tutors."

I folded my arms across my chest. "Uh huh, and how do you suggest I get around the fact that most of them hate me, and those who don't are just stuck at 'tolerating me' until their tires are replaced and they can continue towards hate?"

Billy threw his hands above his head with his fingers fanned out. "You could perform a sultry dance! The dance of the 'Don't hate me, I'm just misunderstood!" He started to pinch his fingers like he was clapping castanets in his hands. I'd showed him once that I knew how to perform flamenco and he never let me live it down.

I started to chuckle. "You're so fucking weird."

"Or ya know," Billy said, returning to normal, "try and shed your title as the school bitch." Easier said than done. It ran through my veins these days.

The doors to the lunchroom opened and the proverbial music in the lunchroom of chatter and eating screeched to a halt. It happened every single day at this exact time; the moment the popular kids progressed to their coveted table and ate lunch amongst us mere mortals. Like any other school, a select group of students, most of them via their involvement in sports, had earned themselves some false notoriety. Orchard Mesa was progressive in that some of the 'nerdier' clubs like Mathletes and Debate had popular representatives as well, having earned the school several accolades, but a majority of the sector was made up of the cheerleaders and the varsity sports teams. This of course meant that, focused right around the middle of the pack, with his even longer brown hair hanging messy and free around his head, was Colin Undinger; head quarterback for the Orchard Mesa varsity football team and the man who'd shattered my heart.

In the five years since we'd last spoken, he'd developed quite a bit of bulk, with full, toned arms and broad shoulders. The already tall 5' 11" he'd been in middle school had spiked to close to well over six feet and he kept an understated goatee on his face. My internal temperature definitely still spiked whenever I saw him. Poor, 12-year-old me couldn't believe how gorgeous her childhood crush had gotten, especially considering the fact that she thought he was gorgeous before he settled into puberty.

He was walking hand-in-hand with Harlie Jones, the football team manager, and a woman most closely associated with the devil. People thought I was evil, but she only ever did things to elevate her own status, including dating the star quarterback. She had a short, black pixie cut and piercing yellow eyes that should have been enough of a clue that she had her pitchfork hidden under her sluttily short skirt.

Colin looked over at me, and I ignored the leap in my heart rate and quickly threw up a middle finger. He scrunched his nose and threw one up to match mine.

Harlie peeked around him and glared at me. "Crawl in a hole and die."

"Oh, are you accepting openings inside your gaping and often-visited vagina?" I shot back quickly.

Colin pulled her back to his side with a roll of his eyes and they walked on.

"Nice." Billy gave me a high-five. "Is today the day you're going to tell me why you hate Colin?"

"Nope." Curiosity finally got the best of me and I reached across and snagged a piece of the yellow concoction on Billy's plate, discovering it was actually some kind of cheesy potatoes.

"Come on," Billy whined. "I know about your," he stuck his hands in the air and made large, dramatic air quotes, "'tutoring.' It can't be worse than that, right?"

I leered at him. "Let it go."

He held up his hands. "Fine."

The rest of the day passed at a snail's pace until I was finally sitting in physics with the clock counting down to the end of the day.

"I know we only have a few minutes left, so please turn to page 196 in your books so we can go over your assignment for the night."

Mr. Val Kepler, the 11th grade physics teacher, gave me a quick glance and I winked back at him, opening my book and turning it to a totally random page. He and I both knew I wouldn't be expected to do the homework on page 196. He was six solid feet of a man who could have been undercover as a high school teacher to study for a role in his next movie, or porno. He had short dark hair in an undercut and a balbo goatee. His eyes were a mysterious gray, and his skin had a natural tan to it. He was stunning. He explained the assignment masterfully, which I challenged him to do while sitting under my lustful gaze, but he didn't flinch. The bell rang, and all of the students packed up their books and followed out of the classroom one by one until only the two of us remained.

"Miss Marquette, was there something I can do

for you?" He sat at his desk and started flipping through a binder, pretending to be uninterested with my presence.

I stood up from my desk, walked over to the door to shut it, even closing the small black shudder that covered the slim, peer-through window. I pressed the button to lock the door and then sauntered my way over to Val's desk. I seated myself on the top, and crossed my legs over one another right next to his head.

"Well, I don't think I'm going to finish tonight's assignment," I hummed. "I was wondering if there was something we could do."

"Unless you're willing to do extra credit, I'm afraid there's nothing we can do." He kept his eyes trained on his binder with impressive focus.

"You're sure?" I lifted my sweater over my head and dropped it to the side of my desk, leaving me in just my black camisole. "Nothing?"

Val looked up at me then, his eyes instantly landing on my large bust forcing my cami to the max. He stood up and placed his arms on either side of me. "Where did you learn to behave this *naughty* young lady?"

I grabbed Val's tie. "I had a good tutor."

Val pressed himself against me, touching his lips to

my cheek before working his way down my neck. A wandering hand glided up my thigh until it could hop up to push at the edge of my cami. I wrapped my arms around Val's neck, feeling the burning inside me churn hotter and hotter. He started to push me back to lay on his desk when my phone cried out from my backpack.

I looked over at it and pushed on Val's shoulder. "My phone."

Val lifted from the place he'd latched onto on my shoulder. "Just ignore it."

"It could be my parents. You know they freak out when I don't answer." Val tried to keep going, but I smacked the back of his head and he stood up with an irritated growl. "Just grab it."

He walked over to my backpack and fished my phone out and handed it to me. It was in fact my parents, and I was only just noticing that they'd actually texted several times before the phone call. "I have to call back."

Val rolled his eyes and slumped back down in his desk chair. "If someone walks in and sees me with a boner, that's on you."

"The door's locked." I dialed my mom's number and waited for her to answer. "Hey mom. Sorry, my phone was still in Do Not Disturb from school."

"Come home immediately." Her voice was shaking and filled with urgency.

"Mom? Are you okay?" I looked at Val and his irritated expression had shifted towards a concerned one.

"I'm okay, but you need to come home immediately. It's an emergency."

## 3

# TATIANA

I hurried down the couple of blocks to my house as fast as I could. My parents never demanded anything of me, so I took their order for me to get home immediately as a bad omen. I unlocked the front door and walked inside, immediately getting rushed by my mom and pulled into a strangling hug.

"Mom." I pushed against her. "Mom, what's wrong? You're scaring me." She stepped back from me and her eyes were red and swollen. I touched her cheek. "Hey. What's going on?"

She took a deep sniffle in with tears quickly rushing in to replace the ones she'd attempted to wipe away. "Ryan Undinger was murdered."

My whole body turned to stone in place. "W-what?"

My mom nodded. "And Helena is in the hospital in critical condition. They were attacked in their restaurant."

My jaw dropped. I looked over her shoulder at my dad who'd snuck his way into the entryway and was standing behind her quietly. His face was equally anguished. "I, um…" I let out a breath. "This is a joke, right?" Tears of my own were gathering in the corners of my eyes.

My mom tugged me back against her, followed by my dad, who wrapped his arms around us both. "It's not," he said sadly.

Ryan and Helena were Colin's parents and two of my parents' closest friends. They'd all gone to high school together and Ryan and my dad played on the Orchard Mesa varsity team together. It had just been common knowledge amongst them that when they eventually had children, those children would become best friends; that was Colin and I. In fact, my dad maintained to this day that my mom didn't want kids until right after she found out Helena was pregnant, after which point she chased the dream until she eventually conceived her own a few months later. I'd spent whole weeks with the Undingers before.

They used to always take me on vacation with them, saying that I was family. They'd been like a second set of parents to me growing up. I suddenly hated myself for not seeing them again even after Colin and I grew apart, and even worse for how Colin and I's separation kept my parents from seeing them as often.

We released from our family hug and walked into the living room where the dreadful story of the burglar who'd broken into the restaurant they owned while it was full of patrons and tried to hold the place up. Ryan, ever fearless, jumped into action to protect his business, customers, and wife, and got shot, while Helena, who tried to finish what her husband had started, was able to disarm the thief, but hit her own head in the process. Ryan was pronounced dead on arrival and Helena was rushed to the hospital where she was still in critical condition, and it wasn't looking good.

My parents held me close as we all sat staring at the television in disbelief. Two people who'd had such a profound effect on my family over the course of the last four decades were suddenly just *gone*. Even once the story was over, we all continued to sit in pained silence until my dad finally got the where-withal to make us something to eat to at least keep sustenance in our bodies as we wept over lost friends. I checked my social media accounts, and it was all anyone was talking about.

"Did Colin post anything?" my mom asked, looking over my shoulder.

I scrolled through my feed, knowing good and well that nothing from him would pop up. We weren't friends on Facebook. "Not that I can see."

My mom's hands were sitting lifeless in her lap. "I can't imagine what he's going through. He's so close with his parents."

My dad was in the kitchen putting together whatever collection of ingredients he'd decided was best for shock and mourning. "His only relative lives in New York, right? Helena's sister. I wonder who he's staying with. There's no way she's made it here yet."

My mom looked to me with her eyes still glistening with sadness. "You should call him. Tell him to come here."

The thought nearly made my skin crawl off my body. "No, mom. I'm not going to do that. We're not really friends anymore."

Her expression turned into one of dignified rage and parental disappointment. "I'm not asking you to invite him to your birthday party, Tatiana. He just lost his father and his mother's in the hospital. You can't visit with people in critical condition.

He could be there all alone. At least call and see if he needs one of us to come down."

"I don't even have his number." I knew it wasn't a good idea to argue with my parents during such a painful time, but they were exactly asking me to do the easiest thing in the world. "I feel bad, but I don't know how to contact him."

"Can't you send him a message on Facebook?" My dad walked over with two bowls in his hand filled with rice, pineapple, glazed chicken, and a medley of veggies.

"We're not friends on Facebook either."

My mom stood up from the couch. "Tatiana. You are making me feel very disappointed to call you my daughter. Where's your compassion? You two used to be thick as thieves, you mean to tell me you aren't the slightest bit worried about his well being?"

I stared at the floor. Of course I was worried. I couldn't even fathom a guess as to how he was handling it. Colin had taken after his father when it came to football. The two used to spend every Sunday afternoon during football season tossing the football around before games, and again after. I used to love sitting in the Undinger's backyard tire swing just watching Ryan and Colin throw the ball back and forth until the palms of their hands were raw. Helena would step out onto their back porch to tell us that dinner was done, and every single time, without fail, Ryan would turn and "surprise" me by hurling the ball at me. Colin would charge forward getting in between it and I, catching it and then flashing me a cocky smile. The looks on their faces the one time I jumped out of the tire swing and caught the ball myself was priceless. Colin called me 'incredible.'

Of course I cared, but I couldn't show it. The second I started to show it, all the pain was going to come back, and I didn't want to deal with it again. "I'm sure he'll be okay."

My mom sucked her teeth and stormed off. My dad sat down on the couch next to me and set the bowl of food in my lap. "Here, eat. It'll help."

I set my head in my hands as a steady flow of tears started to pour from my eyes. The pain of losing Ryan and Helena, the pain of losing Colin, the pain of knowing that Colin must be suffering, was a roaring stampede over me with only my dad's hand on my back, rubbing in a gentle circle, keeping me from getting eaten alive.

Eventually, I made my way up to my room, exhausted from grief and confusion. I kept my eye on social media for updates on Helena as I prayed to any god that would listen that she would be okay.

As I was tracking news posts, I did give in and sneak over to Colin's Facebook page to see if there was any information of note, but it was too flooded with well wishes from others to see anything of substance. I was scrolling aimlessly through everyone's pictures from the Undinger's restaurant which shared their last name when I got a text from Val.

Have you seen all this stuff
about Colin Undinger's parents?

> Yeah. His parents and my parents
> were really close.

Oh shit, seriously? I'm sorry
Tati, I didn't know that. You
hate Colin.

> Yeah. Unrelated. His parents
> were always wonderful to me.

I wish I could hug you and
help.

> I wish you could too…

Could you… No. NVM.

What?

I mean. I know it sounds
like a shitty thing to do, but
if your parents thought you
were coming to a student vigil
or something, would they let you
leave this late? I know they're
hosting them everywhere.

Probably.

Then I could hug you after all.

…I'll see you soon.

I decided to send my parents a text even though we were in the same house. It was better than coming face to face with their disappointment again. I told them that Billy and I were going to go to a vigil that some of the students were hosting and then I was going to spend the night with Billy to be near a friend. My mom didn't respond, but my dad told me to be careful.

They didn't consider Billy a threat. Maybe it was because they thought he was gay, may it was because they knew that, deep down inside of me my heart lied elsewhere, but whatever the reason, they always trusted overnights with Billy and me to be above the board. I chose not to tell them that he'd met some girl from Texas online and was convinced they were going to meet up and get married one day. I felt like that would make them feel worse than just thinking he liked men. I felt like *he* would rather have them think that as well.

I texted Billy the cover story, and after he approved, I got out of bed to get ready. As I packed enough stuff to get me through the night, Colin found his way to my mind. The story as people knew it was that Colin and I hated one another. Ever since we went our separate ways back in middle school, things had just been sour between us. I'd gotten a couple of calls from Colin that night, but I refused to talk to him, and by the time I got to school the next day, he wouldn't even look at me. For a little bit, we just didn't talk to one another, but then at some point we started being outwardly nasty to one another. I don't even remember who started it. We'd make faces at each other, curse each other out, and I even chucked something at him once. The more popular he became, the more people hated me for being at odds with the most popular guy in the school, and soon, we were enemies. Everyone knew it, students, teachers; it was common knowledge, but no one knew why, and if I had a say in it, no one would.

---

When I finally stirred, the clock on Val's nightstand read that it was after midnight. In a habit he'd developed from college, Val didn't often sleep through the night. More often than not, I'd awaken after a night of sex to find that he'd woken up and wandered into his living room to watch TV and do work. I didn't understand how he functioned that way, I was shitty after a full eight hours, let alone only four or five.

I knew exactly where to find his shirts now, unlike the first time I'd ever stayed over. I grabbed one of his button ups, always the sexier choice, and started for the living room, just imagining what my parents would say if they knew where I really was; or anyone for that matter.

I didn't pretend to be oblivious to the taboo of a student sleeping with a teacher, especially when the student was a minor. What we were doing was illegal in all 50 states. I didn't intend to develop as close to 'feelings' as I could develop for Val when I'd first met him the year prior. I'd been bumped up to junior physics because of how far ahead of my peers I was, and asked Val if he'd be willing to tutor me to keep up with the other students who were all a year older than me. He'd agreed and we started putting in after school sessions. He was smart, kind, and gentle, everything a girl looks for; well that and dead-to-rights good looks and a sexual magnetism that could suffocate a room. I was the one who threw myself at Val and when he finally found himself without the ability to resist me, we started up a relationship. Well, as much of a relationship as a 16-year-old student and a teacher could have, which mostly included classroom sex and the occasional lying to parents to spend the night at his house. We couldn't go out together, our town was too small.

I rounded the corner out of the hallway into the living room and could hear the television muttering quietly. I walked over and the second Val saw me, sitting in his big arm chair with only a shirt and sweatpants on, he moved his computer out of his lap and held out his arms.

I walked over and took my seat in his lap, only

then noticing that he was watching a news story covering Colin's parents.

"Did they say anything about Helena?" I asked.

Val's arms closed a little tighter around me. "Yeah… she passed."

# 4

## TATIANA

There was a pall of darkness over the school the next day. I'd arrived early, having had to leave Val's house when he left and have him drop me off a couple of blocks from school so I could walk the rest of the way leaving our relationship undetected. I sat in my first period as people slowly filed in, all wearing black. The entire school was mourning the loss of the Undingers and I was no exception. I wore my own black blouse with billowing sleeves and a pair of black leggings with black riding boots. My dreams had been filled with cheery memories of Ryan, Helena, Colin, and I. Spending summers on varying warm beaches during the Undingers only time off in a year. Sitting around their large, oak dining table, making homemade pizzas; Helena liked to dip her fingers in the pizza sauce and drop it on Colin's nose, which would usually result in him trying to do the same to me. I even dreamed, again, about the day Colin shared our first kiss, but earlier that morning when Ryan and Helena brought brunch from their restaurant over for my parents and I to join them in enjoying before we left for the mall. I remember sitting at that table, laughing along with all of them, thinking to myself that I hoped I'd have a wedding reception with a similar scene one day.

It was no longer the lack of any relationship between Colin and I that would prevent that reality from being realized. The Undingers were gone.

My math teacher walked into the classroom finally as the time to begin first period arrived. She too was wearing a somber black dress, and the typical primary colored bow that encircled the staple bun in her hair, was a dark gray.

Ordinarily she would begin unpacking her materials as soon as she entered, but on this day she didn't. "Ladies and gentlemen. I know I speak for all of us when I say today is not our best day. Our community lost two people who meant a lot to many of us, and I don't expect we'll recover from this loss anytime soon. Classes have been canceled for today. Instead, we will be having an assembly this morning and then law enforcement and student counselors will be available to any of you who think you could use someone to talk to. Your teachers and I will be available as well. A few of your peers are also hosting a fundraiser that will be going on for the bulk of the day. You can order flowers to send to the Undingers' vigil this weekend. 75% of the proceeds from those sales will be placed into a relief fund for the Undingers' son, Colin, who many of you may know. You are welcome to use today however you see fit, but you are, unfortunately, required to stay on campus for the duration of the day, even during lunch. If you have any questions, please ask me, otherwise you may head to the auditorium now."

Students began to gather and walk out, and I could only imagine what bullets of emotions awaited me. It was bad enough that the entire school was acting like they'd lost their own parents and I couldn't even truly mourn the way I wanted to. Most of them only know Ryan and Helena from their restaurant and that was it. The relationship between them and me was vastly different and I didn't quite know how to let that out. Should I cry about it? Should I yell at someone or throw things? Should I do what my parents wanted me to do and try and put Colin and I's differences aside and mourn with him?

I vetoed that idea as soon as it came to me. Ryan and Helena's death was an upsetting situation, but not so upsetting that I could sacrifice the wall I'd worked hard to build between myself and their son. It was there to protect me; it would be irresponsible to just walk around it.

I threaded into the blackened sea of people all funnelling in the same direction and found my eyes wandering through the crowd for Colin without my permission. My anxiety spiked every time I considered how much pain he must be in. I wasn't in any position to help soften the blow, but I guess I just wanted to see him on his own two feet to know he could still stand.

An arm linked with mine as I fought to get through the auditorium's only two doors along with the rest of the school's population. I looked over and Billy was attached to me, wearing a black, button up shirt, and dark jeans.

"This is insane." His voice was low, as if he didn't want anyone else to hear what they all must have been thinking. "I mean, you can throw a rock from one end of Orchard Mesa to the other. Can you believe someone so heinous was here? Thank god they got him."

Word had broken early in the morning that the assailant hadn't wasted his time in seeking a plea deal after being arrested by the police. Things moved quickly in Orchard Mesa because serious crimes were sparse, but even that was probably a town record. Apparently the criminal felt bad; he didn't intend for anyone to get hurt. I suppose when you're looking for a quick come up and end up staring down two murders, you regret your life choices pretty quickly, but I almost would have felt better if he was a stone cold killer who didn't care. Just because he wanted a few quick bucks, I'd never get to see two people who meant so much to me? And he gets to be remorseful and turn over a new leave in prison while my entire town is in shambles?

Fuck that guy.

"Tati?" Billy pulled me a little closer to him and tipped his head to mine. "I know, death is hard."

At first I didn't know what had elicited that response from him, but then the soft feeling of tears running down my face alerted me that I was crying. When had I started? It was all weighing so heavily on my mind, and I wasn't even sure I had the right to be sad. That wound was far-wider than the others.

"I knew them really well," I murmured. "The Undingers."

Billy's eyes widened as we finally needled into the auditorium and found a couple of seats near the back. "What? You did? But you hate Colin."

"I didn't, at one time." I wasn't sure why the story was coming out all of a sudden. It was this horrible, blood-sucking leech on my chest that I was desperate to pull off, even if it took a gallon of my blood with it. "I was in love with him."

Billy's eyes widened. "Shut up. Are you serious? You guys are awful to each other."

"Our parents had been best friends since high school, so when they had kids, they just sort of forced them together. Damn near every day, for 12 years, I spent my days with Colin. He was my best friend, my first kiss, and my first heartbreak." My hands started to shake as I realized I'd never said it out loud before. I'd written it down, I'd thought it to myself, over and over, but the words had never crossed my lips.

"God, I don't know if this," he motioned to the school's makeshift memorial of two portraits and a few bouquets of flowers, "or this," he motioned to me, "is more shocking."

I sniffed in, trying to keep myself from trudging into an all-out sob. I didn't like showing emotions. "They were like parents to me too, but I didn't speak to them once in the last five years. All because their son is an asshole. I wouldn't even go to their restaurant." Billy put his arm around my back and I dipped my head in, placing it on the back of the seat in front of me. "Helena's three cheese penne was like my *favorite* food in the world. Every time I came into the restaurant, she would make me this huge batch, enough to eat and to take home. I think it was so good to me because she made it."

My throat burned and chest tightened and nose ran. I was a single person running around trying to block up all the holes letting emotions flood in, and I wasn't doing a very good job. "You should talk to one of the counselors," Billy suggested.

I shook my head. "I don't want to talk to anyone. I just want to go home."

I didn't say anything else through the presentation our principal gave to the school honoring the Undingers. I only barely heard that Colin would be taking the day off, but that students were encouraged to reach out to him with well wishes, before I shoved my headphones in my ear, curled up against Billy and checked out. He tapped me on my shoulder once the service had ended to let me know that the teachers were all headed back to their classrooms for students who needed it. I thanked him for comforting me, asked him not to share my story, not that he had anyone to share it with, and beelined for Val's classroom.

It wasn't surprising to see that there was a small group of students gathered inside, sitting in the front row of desks, listening while Val talked them through their grief. He didn't have a skill set for it, but Val's tongue was one of his gifts, in more ways than one. He could talk the devil into buying a barbecue.

When I walked in, he noticed me immediately, putting on a sad, half-smile. "Miss Marquette."

"Um... Can I talk to you?"

"Of course." He looked at the other students. "Sorry, this is the pre-arranged appointment I told you all about. Give us fifteen minutes and you're welcome back."

Leave it up to Val to have prepared an out just in case I came by. If I were walking a stronger stride I might be annoyed that I was being so predictable, but really I just wanted some comfort, and a free pass to go home.

The students filed out, each of them shooting me varying glares of dissatisfaction.

"I know, you all hate me. That bit is old," I snapped as they passed, causing one girl to jump.

"Tatiana," Val warned.

I stepped off to the side and let the students

pass and then I shut and locked the door. Val walked over to me and wrapped an arm around my back. He ducked down to kiss me, but I turned my head, not feeling very affectionate at the moment. He grabbed my chin and corrected it, lining my lips up to his. I sighed as he did so, not wanting to argue, and returned the kiss.

I pulled away sooner than I might have in any other situation, looking up at Val through sad eyes. "I gotta get out of here. I can't take all this…" I was flailing my arms, hoping to find purchase on any single word to accurately describe my influx of emotions. "…this."

"Go home. I'll take care of it." Val pet my head as he said so and I was hoping that was what he would say. "I'll text you later."

I nodded. "Okay."

I turned to walk out, but Val grabbed my hand and turned me to face him. He stared down at me through pointed gray eyes. "I wanted to tell you this yesterday, but it never came up." He brought my hand to his mouth and placed a peck on the back. "I love you." I didn't know what to do or say or do. I'd honestly never considered love when I thought of Val. I'd never considered it when I thought of anyone, I'd really written off the whole concept after Colin. "You don't have to say anything now, I know you're hurting. I just thought it might help to know how I feel. A little light in the darkness."

"Y-yeah." The speed I used to get away from Val felt like it might leave a me-shaped hole in his classroom door with a cartoonish 'pew' humming in my wake.

All the students and teachers were too distracted to notice me as I raced for the door, but I turned the final corner and came face to face with an unfair obstacle; Harlie standing behind a gray table with a cash box in front of her, and a piece of white poster board reading 'Honorary Undinger Recovery Fund.'

I wished I was wearing a hoodie. There was a reason I wore clothes I could hide in, there was nothing to pull over my head and hide me from Harlie's evil stare. I tried to just slink past her, but I might have known that it wouldn't be that easy.

"And where do you think you're going?" I sighed and turned to face her and her arms were crossed in front of her. "We're supposed to stay on campus."

"I have permission, not that I owe you an explanation of any kind." I tried to continue on, but Harlie walked around the table and stood between me and the front door. "God, I really don't want to hit you on a day like today."

"Maybe you'd be interested in investing in the recovery fund?" There was an hissing insinuation to her voice that, if I didn't, she'd squeal. "One bouquet is only $20."

"I don't have any money." Once more, I tried to push around her, but she stepped to the side, keeping herself in my path.

She put her hands on her hips. "Really? You always have plenty during lunch."

"Good to know you study me," I replied.

"Please, I couldn't begin to have the time. I always have to get Colin's attention."

The thought knocked me off center. "What?"

"He hates you so much that he just sits there staring at you. It's sad. He told me you two used to be good friends. How could you turn into such an evil person towards him, someone who cared about you? His parents would probably be pretty disappointed."

I pictured myself throttling her until she blacked out, but I didn't want to make anymore trouble on a day already overflowing with trouble. "Keep your fucking mouth shut. You have no idea what you're talking about." I shoved her aside and started for the door.

"You two dated, didn't you?" I stopped short and she scoffed. "I knew it." I turned around and looked at her, suddenly curious to where she'd gathered her ideas. "He got drunk once and told me about his 'one true love.' I thought he was talking about me, but he said it was before me. Tell me, Tatiana, were you and Colin ever more than friends?"

With each word, I felt more like a fly getting battered to death against a zapper. "Mind your own business."

I turned on my heel and started back towards Val's classroom. One true love? Staring at me during lunch? Who did he think he was? *He* was the one who rejected *me*. He was the one who went to school two days after we first kissed and flirted with a girl right out in the open like I wouldn't see. What right did he have to act like that?

I stormed into Val's classroom where the same set of students had returned and were talking with Val. "Get out," I growled. They all stared back at me like they weren't prepared to listen, and I wasn't prepared to hold my temper. "What? Are all of you the same level of fucking dumb? Get out! Now!"

"Tatiana!" Val yelped.

I started swiping towards the door. "Come on. We don't want to see me get any nastier than this. Out. Please."

Val looked apologetically at the students. "Just give us a few more minutes."

The students stood up, a litany of swear words hurtling at me, not that I cared. "Yeah, yeah, yeah." The last student out the door probably got impaled on the knob.

Val crossed his arms. "I know you're upset, but you can't just behave like--"

"I love you too."

Val swallowed. "What?"

I lifted my blouse over my head and threw it to the side. "I love you too, and I want you. Right now."

Val shook his head. "I don't know, Tati. That's pretty risky."

I started to undo my bra. "I could use a little risk."

## 5

## TATIANA

After Val and I finished my anger-induced romp, I had him walk me out the front door to keep Harlie's dumb mouth shut. When I was out in the open air, I took a deep breath in and held it until it felt like I may pass out. I teased the idea, thinking it might be so much easier to just blackout and let the rest of the day carry on without me, but my lungs started to burn, and I caved, letting the air out and recovering my breath.

"You're going straight home?" Val asked.

I nodded. "Yeah, and probably right to bed."

He smirked. "I would imagine, after *that*."

I squeezed his hand before letting it go and then started off towards my house. I had more than one regret. I didn't love Val. What I felt towards him was *mostly* sexual with a side of emotional-support when I couldn't get a hold of Billy and my parents wouldn't understand. It was unfair to us both that I'd allowed Harlie's stories to get to me and inspire me to say something I didn't mean, but there was no taking it back. I resigned myself to just fall in love with him, whatever that meant. To make the words true, then I would undo the mistake I made by saying them in the first place. If they were true, but maybe uttered sooner than they should have been, that changed it from something only horrible women did to a fun story you tell your kids over Thanksgiving when they're old enough. That was the new plan, to make what I'd said true.

It was a good thing my house was only a couple of blocks away because after the hard and fast sex I'd demanded from Val to try and shove away my feelings, walking was more of a task than it should have been. It was only just before noon and neither of my parents got home from work until after 5. Not only would they not know I skipped and wonder why they never got a truancy call, but I could have a nice, long soak in the massive, jacuzzi tub in my parent's master bathroom before crawling into bed.

My headphones were nestled inside my ears, playing through all of my favorite songs, until one came on that shifted me dramatically. It was the song that was the number one hit the day Colin and I went to the mall and he first kissed me. Due to its popularity at the time, it had played several times throughout the day, so when I got home, that day, I immediately bought it. It just so happened to be a cheesy love song, so when I played it on repeat until I fell asleep, I thought of Colin and, what I'd hoped, would be our new relationship. Every time it played now, I would fly to my phone to delete it, not liking the memories it brought, but just like my feelings for Colin, I could never quite bring myself to get rid of it. As the lyrics swirled around me, I touched the, now bare spot on my collarbone where the locket I'd bought used to hang. Even though I only wore it for a little under two days, I found myself touching the spot absent-mindedly, as if it was the one piece of my body that was still clinging hopelessly to those sweet times.

I dropped my hand and skipped the song. No. Now was not the time to go back to the 'good ol' days.' They hadn't ended up that good anyway. I tried to force my mind back to taking a bath and going to bed, likely the only things that were going to bring me solace today.

I allowed the idea of relaxation to carry me through the crisp afternoon air, until I got to my house and my dream was shattered. Not just one, but both of my parents' cars were in the driveway. They were both home in the middle of the day? Why?

I walked up to my door, preparing myself to face the rain of accusations I was about to be faced with. The door wasn't locked, so I opened it and slipped inside, halfway planning to sneak upstairs before I was noticed. I'd have to skip my bath for the time being, but if I could at least hide my presence for a few hours, I could make it seem like I didn't skip. It was all a pipe dream though, as the second I opened the door, my mom came walking into the hallway.

"Tatiana. Why aren't you at school?" she asked. I opened my mouth to respond, but she waved her hand through the air. "It doesn't matter. It's a good thing you're here. Come."

She turned and led back through the doorway opposite the front door, into the kitchen. I took off my shoes, dropped my backpack on the stairs, and followed after her. I rounded the corner, unsure of what to expect was awaiting me, but when I discovered what it was, I froze.

Colin held up his hand, offering a barely-there smile. "Hey, Tatiana."

I looked at my dad and my dad looked back at

me and I looked over at my mom and my mom looked back at me and then I looked at Colin. He was simply dressed in jeans and t-shirt, and had clearly been crying recently. My heart was blending my stomach at max speed and I felt like the single piece of toast I'd eaten that morning was going to be making a return trip.

"What's going on?" I asked.

"Remember yesterday when I said that Colin's only living relative lives in New York? He's under 18, so they tried to get him to move there with her. he wants to finish out his schooling so…"

No.

"…we've offered for him to stay here with us until he graduates."

My mom wrapped her arm around my shoulders. "Looks like you two are going to have to figure out how to be friends again."

## 6

# COLIN

I t had been another night of no sleep. I didn't have much left in me, and was still struggling to figure out how one adjusts to losing their parents suddenly, especially when being shoved into the face of a former love turned enemy. I should be grateful to Kya and Cristiano for taking me in, I was, but the fact remained that being under the same roof as Tatiana for the rest of the school year was far from the rest and reprieve from my current misfortune that I was hoping for.

I didn't really have anyone to blame but myself. I didn't have many friends. Well, I didn't have many real friends. I had going out friends. Meet up at the movies in a huge group friends. Make stupid jokes on each other's social media pages friends, but the only person in my life I'd ever trusted fully and allowed into my life was Tatiana, and she'd quickly shown me that was a huge mistake.

Maybe I'd just misread things. I thought that over a year of holding hands, going out on, what I thought were dates, and then finally sharing our first kiss after she gave me a really thoughtful gift meant we were on the road to being together. Her saying being my girlfriend would be 'gross' and throwing her half of the locket we'd split at my feet suggested otherwise. I was like a puppy who couldn't wait to show its owner the stick it found the day I saw I'd made the A-team. People were surrounding me and asking me all sorts of questions and trying to get to know me, and I was just phoning it in until I could get to the one I really wanted to be with; the one I loved.

That joke was on me.

I took both halves of the locket and shoved them and my feelings as far back in my sock drawer as they would go.

Somewhere along the way of the past five years I probably should have accepted that preteens over-dramaticized everything, so the life-ending pain I felt when Tatiana rejected me was nothing more than a boy going through his first heartbreak and I'd have many *real* loves as I got older, but Tatiana was different. Our love wasn't just two middle schoolers who randomly decided we had a crush on each other because we thought the other was cute. I'd known Tatiana as long as I'd known my own parents. She was the one constant I'd always had in my life, and I couldn't think back to a day when I didn't wake up excited to go and see her. Little six-year-old me only wanted to share my toys with her and eight-year-old me had to be convinced that things were true by her alone. Only Tatiana's words were true to me regardless. She was a religion to me, the one thing I believed in above all things. Her smile, her laugh, her pout when she lost games, her quick wit and tendency to be over analytical. There wasn't a thing she did that I didn't absolutely adore. She was my everything.

And then one day she wasn't.

All of a sudden, I had to wake up knowing I wasn't going to see her. I couldn't share with her and I couldn't listen to her convince me things were true. Someone could have taken my left lung and caused less damage. I'd built everything on Tatiana, so when that foundation split and left me a pile of rubble, I couldn't be bothered to build it up again. If I didn't rebuild it, there was nothing to break.

Slowly, but surely, Tatiana and I grew to hate each other. I never understood where things had gone wrong with us, and any attempt to find out was met with resistance, so eventually I just stopped trying. I went tit for tat with her. Everything she did, I did it twice, at least sparring was still contact. She'd start a rumor, I'd start a worse one. She'd curse me out, I'd blast her on social media. I wanted to be a presence in her life, if even an irritating one. If she never forgot me only because I became someone she loathed, then at least I could sleep knowing I left *some* impression on her. Not the one I wanted, but such is life.

It took a true twisted and unstable individual to be just as concerned about sleeping across from his former best friend, and the love of his life, than he was about the recent death of his parents. At least I knew what happened with my parents, Tatiana Marquette was just a big ass question mark.

"Colin?" Tatiana's mom, Kya, knocked on my door from outside. "Are you awake? Are you hungry?"

I climbed out of the bed and walked over to the door, opening it and eliciting a startle out of Kya. "Oh, I'm sorry, I didn't mean to scare you."

"No." Kya shook her head. "Tati always just yells back at me from the other side of her door, so I guess it caught me off guard."

"I can hear you!"

Tatiana's voice amplified from the room across the hall and covered me in goosebumps. She was so close. I was staying in the room that used to be our playroom. The outline of my name was even still marked on the wall from where Tatiana and I had stuck stickers against her mom's warning not to and got in huge trouble. Her dad eventually designed the playroom around the adhered names. I wondered when they removed them?

Kya smiled and ignored her daughter's jab. "Cristiano is going to make breakfast burritos I think. Would you like one? Tati never eats before school."

"I can *still* hear you!"

"That sounds good, thank you." I glued on as realistic a smile as I could muster.

She nodded. "Okay. Are you thinking school today, or do you still want to take another day?"

"I want to go today. It's not really doing me any good to just sit around." I attempted to feed my fingers through my long, brown hair, but they snagged in several places. I'd neglected my personal hygiene a little too much for my comfort. I probably didn't have much time before school today, but the evening would have to be one of grooming myself. "Thanks."

"Okay, well Cristiano usually brings Tati, so I'm

sure you can steal a ride." She grinned. She was trying *very* hard to make things feel normal. It wasn't working, but I appreciated the effort. "Just come on down when you're ready."

"I will, thanks."

Kya skittered off down the hallway and I just stood staring at Tatiana's door. It was dreadful knowing she was just on the other side. What would she do if I just walked in? In the past it would have been welcomed, but it felt like it had invisible bars in front of it now. I returned to 'my' room and dressed myself in something that seemed at least marginally normal, tossed my hair into a bun at the top of the back of my neck, and headed downstairs.

Staying in the old playroom was tough enough, but walking through Tatiana's house was torture. Every piece of peeling paint held memories. I walked down the stairs remembering us sitting there back in the 2nd grade. Tatiana had developed her first crush on a boy in her class and he gave her some of his chips, but then offered some to another girl, and she was devastated. I'd gone out with my dad that night and bought her two big bags of chips and brought them over to her house the next day.

I walked past her living room where we used to

hole up for hours building the Taj Mahal of living room forts. It was her birthday, and I was the only one who had the honor of getting invited. We used everything at our disposal: pillows, blankets, chairs, and Tatiana was so intelligent, she designed it a way that made the barred backs of the chairs we used look like windows. She draped sheets over that we could pull shut when we wanted the windows 'closed' and she forced her dad to 'deliver' all of her birthday presents, which I then had to go and collect, I was the king after all, and the king always gets presents for the queen.

Little did she know how prepared I was to do that forever.

I walked into the kitchen and saw the island where her parents, my parents, her, and I sat and laughed over the brunch my parents and I brought over. Later that day we went to the mall and Tatiana bought a locket with the allowance money she'd saved up for over a year, and gave me one half of the pendant. She said she picked it out because I loved football. We sat outside at the fountain waiting for my parents to come and pick us up, and her face shining in the sunset and the locket dangling around her neck, matching the one I had; it was too much. I kissed her. I didn't think anything could make me more excited to see if I'd made the football team that Monday, but I was so much more excited to see her. I was going to ask her to be my girlfriend and that was going to be it.

Happy with my parents, happy with Tatiana; all of that was gone. I had nothing.

I was hunched over the sink and retching the next moment I was aware of. Cristiano was next to me on one side, already running the kitchen sink water to help pass some of the bile I'd given up, and Kya was rubbing my back gently.

"It's okay, sweetie, we're here." Kya's voice was comforting, but not cleansing. I just felt like I was putting on cologne when I hadn't bathed. It made no difference. "Let it out. It's okay."

When I was confident I was done, I leaned back, wiping the sour taste from my mouth. Cristiano handed me over a bottle of water, which I graciously took, and downed in a single burst. I just happened to glance over, and I saw Tatiana standing in the entryway of the hallway near the front door. I could only imagine how it must have looked; to see the man she couldn't stand being doted on by her parents. She rolled her eyes, through her backpack over her shoulder and walked out, slamming the door behind her.

"I feel bad," I admitted.

Kya flicked her hand in that direction. "Don't worry about her, she'll be fine."

"Still, I lost my parents already, I don't want Tatiana to feel like she's losing hers." Both Kya and Cristiano seemed taken with the notion, but nodded in understanding.

Kya tilted her head. "Since we never could get it out of Tatiana, can you tell us what came between you two?"

I looked over at the front door. "I honestly can't."

## 7

## COLIN

For it to only be two days, the rest of the week at school sapped me of all of my energy. I knew people were just trying to be nice and considerate of my situation, but everyone being hypersensitive of me pissed me off. It would have been so much nicer to have everyone going about business as usual, not having completely random people walking up to me and giving me all manner of gifts from food to money. I just wanted to act like things were okay for a couple of days before my parents' funeral, but teachers and students alike were intent on reminding me that my parents had died at every waking turn, as if it wasn't something I wore on me every single day.

To make matters worse, things were even more

difficult back at home. When Tatiana wasn't flat out ignoring me, we were scrapping like cats and dogs. A lot of what we fought about weren't actually things we disagreed on, we were just doing it to spite each other, and we both knew it. Despite this, to try and push a 'family agenda,' Tatiana's parents were hellbent on making us have dinner together. For the second night in a row, we were sitting down at the dining room table in awkward silence while Cristiano doled out dishes that were way too delicious for the circumstances they were being consumed in.

Tatiana rolled her eyes as Kya dished up my plate like a helpless seven year old and I nearly blew my stack. What was so wrong that her parents were decent people who didn't treat people like trash? That they just wanted to make sure that I was doing okay in the aftermath of a terrible, life-altering event that I would probably never get over? That at the very least hers were walking around while mine were six feet under? I wanted to shout at her to grow up and stop being such a brat, but I didn't have the energy to knuckle up with her, so I just left it alone.

"I learned this recipe from your mother," Cristiano announced after a full ten minutes of silence.

My mom was a chef. She'd always loved

cooking as a little girl, and as she got older, she went out of her way to learn the craft so that by the time she was graduating from high school, she had already been asked to join several of the most prestigious internships from around the world, including one that was all the way in Japan. To hear my parents tell it, she didn't even think twice about turning them all down. She was already madly in love with my dad, and wanted to stay in Colorado so as not to disrupt their relationship. She and Cristiano were as close as Tatiana and I used to be, so both my father and Cristiano had gotten the benefits of being so close with a chef. Cristiano developed my mom's love for food and cooks more in his household than Kya, who lends herself more to housework on the claim that she wasn't a good cook. Anything she ever made for me was pretty good, so I always assumed she just didn't enjoy it the way Cristiano did.

My mom decided when she was 25 that she wanted to open a restaurant in Orchard Mesa, and my father proposed to her the day she bought the land on which it would be built, inspiring Undinger's, for the name. It had been so successful that many investors tried to offer her tons of money to expand it to the rest of Colorado and eventually the country, but just as she had the internships, she turned them down. She didn't want to leave Orchard Mesa, she didn't even want to have reasons to travel for long periods of time. She said that Orchard Mesa was her home and that's where she'd stay. Eventually, Undinger's became a famous restaurant with "five star food in a three star atmosphere" that could only be found right in our little corner of the world. It was her pride and joy.

She was gone now, and suddenly I had to decide what to do with it. I didn't have an affinity for cooking like my mom, and wasn't sure I had what it took to run a "hands-off" business. Couple this with the fact that I'd previously been counting down the days until I could leave Colorado, and I had myself a regular comedy of errors.

"Her Korean barbecue was always my favorite." Kya took a big bite as she said it, as though she had to convince me.

"Everything she made was my favorite," Cristiano responded.

I sat there watching them volley. It was one of the strategies I was certain they'd been armed with by my designated caseworker to help 'ease' me into a life without my parents. Remember them for the good not the bad. I appreciated what they were going for, but with Tatiana still sitting at the other end of the table trying to set me on fire with her glare, I really just wanted to get up and walk away.

"Um." Kya eyed Cristiano nervously as she started. "So, I know your parents' funeral is tomorrow, and your aunt is in town and was planning to take you with her, but I was wondering if you would be more comfortable going with us? I know that you don't know her very well, and maybe having a few familiar faces at your side would be better?" She shook her head. "I don't know. It's totally up to you."

Tatiana set her fork down next to her plate. Her malicious stare was gone, leaving a look of anguish behind. I thought she was about to puke all over the table. "I'm, um..." She looked at her mom and then her dad. "I don't think it's a good idea for me to go, so, I'm not going to."

Both Cristiano and Kya's heads whipped in her direction like she'd just announced she was pregnant. "What?" they both said, and even Cristiano's voice had heat behind it, which it never did.

"You absolutely are going," Cristiano instructed. "Ryan and Helena were nothing but good to you. You owe it to them."

Tatiana's jaw went a little slack. "I hadn't talked to them in like five years. I'm sorry, it just didn't seem like I should be there taking up space."

Kya slammed her hands on the table. "Now I have had just about enough of you acting like we didn't raise you right. It's not about the quantity, it's about the quality."

Tatiana threw her hand out at me. "It's not like he wants me there anyway? What am I going to do, go sit there and force myself to cry so I fit in with everyone else?"

"Tatiana stop it right now." Cristiano's brows were very low now, closer to anger than I'd ever seen him.

"Why? I'm so sick of tiptoeing around everywhere. I'm sorry that this happened, but I don't understand why all of a sudden I have to be in all these situations that make me uncomfortable." She crossed her arms. "I'm not going."

It was an odd sensation having rage coursing through me as madly as a roaring river, yet not having any ability to draw it forth the way I wanted to. "I'm so sorry you're being inconvenienced by my parents murder, Tatiana. Truly. I wish that this wasn't ruining your day." My voice was somehow dull and sharp. "It really sucks when the people you love certainly aren't there anymore."

Tatiana stared back at me plain faced. "You would know."

"Tatiana!" Kya snapped.

I slid my chair back. "I don't need to deal with this. Thank you both for being so wonderful to me. I'm sorry that you're stuck with this hellspawn!" I stood up. "You were right about one thing, Tati. I *don't* want you at my parents' funeral. I wouldn't want it to be stormed by your minions. In fact, why don't you all skip it? I don't want to cause you anymore stress."

With Cristiano and Kya calling out after me, I grabbed my backpack, and I left. I didn't know where to go. My aunt was staying at a hotel in the city, but it was over an hour away. Besides, she was dealing with making all the arrangements I couldn't and I didn't want to add to her plate. I called Harlie a couple of times, but she didn't answer. I figured, worst case scenario, I could sleep on the porch in her family's backyard and started to walk over. She didn't live far from the Marquettes, and after about 20 minutes, I was standing in front of her house. I was going to just head up to the door and knock when a car pulled up in front of the house. There was a man I didn't recognize in the driver's seat, but Harlie was next to him in the passenger's.

I watched as Harlie climbed out of the car, but turned and leaned back through the window. She was wearing a low cut t-shirt and a flannel shirt over it with her hair and makeup done the same way she did whenever she and I went out. I couldn't make out what she was saying to the man in the car, but clocked every time she forced out a giggle, and then eventually, in an oddly more painful display than I was expecting, she leaned in and kissed the driver. His hand landed on her breast, which he squeezed as she laughed, before they finally parted and he drove away. I waited for Harlie to get inside her house before pulling out my phone and sending her a text.

Lose my number. We're over.

What? Why?
I'm calling you right now.
Stop ignoring my calls.
Colin. Answer your phone.
Hey!! Talk to me!

*Not interested.*

I put my phone away and just started off down the sidewalk. Right as I was turning the corner, Harlie bolted out of her house and started to look all around, expecting that I must have seen her transgression. I didn't break stride and got away without her seeing me. If she sweated over it for the rest of her life, I wouldn't care.

*Why is this happening to me again?*

I definitely didn't know where I was going now. Maybe I'd just keep walking until something hit me and took me out.

# 8

## TATIANA

My head and heart were battling it out for which one could pound against my bones harder. My dad, the peacekeeper of our home, had left to go find Colin, and I was just sitting at the table under the harsh and intense gaze of my mom. The look of disappointment in her eyes was nothing compared to the way I wanted to reach inside my only body and pull my spine out through my throat. I'd officially taken things too far, I knew that. Being mean to Colin was a defense mechanism, and having lost his parents and not quite knowing how to process that, upgraded that mechanism to its 2.0 version, now complete with words no one should ever say, even to an enemy.

"You need to start talking right now." My mom's voice was as low as I ever heard it.

It had a quiver to it, but one that let me know she was trying her damnedest not to crack me over the head with her dinner plate. I couldn't even imagine how it made her and my dad feel to watch me act like I had absolutely zero home training and went to school to learn how to act even more like an idiot. Apologies wouldn't suffice, they should just trade me in for Colin, and I could dropout and go live with my illegal boyfriend.

"Tatiana. Explain yourself."

"I don't know, mom." I pushed my dinner away because the sight of it was churning my stomach. "I don't…" I dropped my head to the table. "I don't know why I said that. I don't even recognize myself."

I heard the screech of my mom's chair across the wood floor as she moved it closer to me. She pet my head in that sweet, make you cry sort of mom way. "What's going on, baby? You have *never* acted like this before. I mean, goodness, if you'd asked me where I thought you and Colin were going to be in five years, I would never have predicted this."

A knot made a home in my throat. "I wouldn't have either."

"That's what he said." Her voice sounded perturbed.

I lifted my head. "What do you mean?"

"Well, I asked him the same question, why you two stopped being friends, and he said that he honestly didn't know."

I sneered. "Sure."

"Talk to me, Tatiana. What happened?"

I looked over at her and could see the curiosity and mom-need to know so she could help. Talking to Billy about Colin had been difficult enough. I wasn't sure I had it in me to tell my mom too. Still, if I was going to continue to act like the devil incarnate, it probably would be helpful for her to know where it all was coming from. I used to talk to my mom about everything. I remembered thinking she was going to try and force reconciliation for her own friendship with Colin's parents, and avoiding telling her because of it. As painful as it was, that wasn't so much an issue anymore.

"You remember that Saturday that I went to the mall with Colin? His parents dropped us off?"

"Vividly," she replied. "Your father and I became pretty convinced after that day that you two were going to start dating. You came home with this huge smile plastered on your face and it was clear that something good had happened, well better than typical for you two. That Monday it was the same; you put on your Sunday best, you did your hair and makeup, but you came home an entirely different person."

"Colin kissed me, at the mall. I bought that locket," my hand drifted subconsciously to the spot on my chest, "and when I gave it to him, he was so happy that he kissed me."

"I would expect that would make you happy?"

A few tears jailbroke my eyes. "It did. It was the best day ever. I loved him so much so when he finally did it, I was like 'Yes!'" I thought of poor, innocent, young me. No idea what was coming up the pike. "I went to school that day so excited because I thought for sure that we were gonna, you know, become boyfriend and girlfriend, but when I got there, he was flirting with someone else. She asked him to Sadie Hawkins and he said that they could maybe go together." I closed my eyes, trying to escape the memory, but it only became more vibrant. "I was heartbroken. I thought he liked me too, but I guess he just thought it was nice to kiss me because I gave him the locket? I don't know."

"Ah," my mom said knowingly. "Your first heartbreak."

"I guess I kind of thought we'd be together forever and I never really got over it. I just never understood why I wasn't good enough." I wrapped my arms around my stomach, the little bit of dinner I had eaten revving up. "And now Ryan and Helena and... I should have stayed in touch. It wasn't their fault. Now I'll never..." I started to sob.

"Oh, baby." My mom rubbed my back more and I just cried. As shitty as it felt, it was a huge release. I wasn't trying to plug the leaks anymore, I was exhausted from trying. "You know, first loves are a dangerous thing, especially when they happen when you're young. You haven't experienced the harshness of adulthood that warns you against giving too much all at once, and you jump all-in. When that comes back to bite you, it can be very difficult to bounce back from. You wouldn't be the first person cursed by the shadow of the first person you ever loved." She spoke like it was from experience, but I didn't want to delve. "You can't just bottle these things up. Helping you get through it is part of my job description, you know?"

I nodded. "Yeah." I finally blinked my eyes open. "I don't know how to apologize."

"Just start with the words, and if you mean it, he'll feel it." She rubbed my cheek. "Maybe on Sunday after this difficult week, you and I can go for lunch and pedicures, just us. How does that sound."

I nodded, sniffling in my tears. "It sounds amazing."

"Then it's settled." She made an awkward face. "Er... Do we invite Billy?"

I let out a tear-stained laugh. Confirmed, they thought he was gay. "I don't think he'd enjoy it."

She nodded, almost relieved. "Okay, because we can."

"It's okay mom," I tapped her hand, "thanks."

Before either of us could say anything else, we heard the front door opening. "Cris?" my mom called out.

"And Colin," my dad shouted back and my chest got tighter.

"Can you both come in here. Only for a moment." She looked over at me and I nodded back at her, sitting up and making my best attempt to wipe my sorrow from my face.

My dad and Colin stepped through the kitchen, into the dining room, and I could plainly see that Colin had done some shedding of tears of his own. I wondered what he talked about with my dad. Did he really not have any idea why I would be so upset that day five years ago? Was he seriously just operating on the belief that one day we were friends and the next day we weren't? Were men seriously that dense?

"Um," I started and my mom grabbed my hand for support. "I'm sorry, Colin." As much as it hurt, I locked myself into his emerald eyes and forced myself to stay there for the duration of the apology. I know that, um… I just, I guess…" I grumbled out of frustration.

"Don't force it." Colin held up a hand. "It's fine."

"No!" I yelped and everyone jumped a little. "I *am* sorry. I guess I just don't know what to say. I had no right to treat you like that. I, uh. I miss them too, so, I think I'm just not dealing with it all that well. I shouldn't have lashed out at you."

Colin blinked and for the first time since he started staying with us, I saw life behind his eyes. "Oh. Thanks. I guess that makes sense, you were close too. They loved you like a daughter."

That notion had tears gathering in my eyes again, but I tried my best to keep them at bay. "I'm sorry for what you must be going through. I can't promise I'll be… good, but I can promise to try harder."

A gentle grin appeared on Colin's face. "I'll take it."

My mom leaned forward in her chair. "Sweetie,

I know that what you're going through is very hard and we," she grabbed my hand, "all of us, just want to help. If you really don't want us to be at the funeral, we can stay back, but…"

Colin held a hand out. "No, I…" he looked at my dad and he nodded back. "I told Cris that I think I really need you guys there." His eyes landed on me again. "All of you."

I nodded. "Then we'll be there."

His smile got a little bigger and it made my world a little brighter. Five years since last smiling at Colin felt like decades. "Thanks, Tati."

My dad tapped Colin's back. "I'll pack up dinner for lunches tomorrow."

My mom stood up. "Come on, I'll walk you guys up."

"We're okay," I responded, not entirely expecting it myself. "I mean, we can just walk up."

My mom was smiling now too. "Okay. Let me know if you need anything."

I walked around the table and as I passed Colin, I stopped and looked up at him. He was staring back at me and something linked between us. I didn't like the feeling of it, like harpoons shooting out and latching into me once again. I broke the connection and continued towards the stairs, feeling him close behind me. My chest was a concert of thumps knowing that Colin was right on my heels, in my house, feet from my room. Young me was jumping up and down, trying to get my attention, but I was ignoring her. Things weren't the same, little me. Sorry.

We got to the parallel doors that led to our rooms. I turned to face him, with not much at all to say. I couldn't even figure what someone *would* say in that situation. I started to study the stucco spots on the ceiling, standing there in silence.

Colin opened his mouth and my eyes shot to him, but then his lips closed again. What was he going to say?

Finally, I had to break the silence and get out of there. It was winding up my anxiety. "Goodnight."

Colin nodded. "Goodnight."

Our eyes locked again, and it was like I was teleported through time to that day at the mall. The sweetness between us was there, exactly as it had been back then. I didn't know how to face it. What was it trying to tell me? How could he sit and look at me like that? A ghost of my logical self finally took control of my body and led it into my bedroom and safely behind the door.

It was beginning to look like Colin Undinger was back to cause my life disruption once again.

## 9

## COLIN

I couldn't have been dreading the day more if I tried. I didn't want to go to my parents' memorial service. It wasn't like I didn't want to celebrate their life, I just didn't want to have to come face-to-face with the fact that they were really and truly gone. They'd been cremated after donating their organs, so at least it wasn't an open-casket, but it was still going to be an amplified version of what I'd already experienced at school. People being solicitous of me, waiting on me, coming up to me to tell me stories of my parents as they held back tears, apologizing for the misfortune I'd endured and offering me support that I didn't want. I was trying to get to the place where I was remembering my parents for the virtuous, amazing people they were, and not being forced to think every single day about how some selfish man had robbed me of them simply because he felt like it.

The Marquettes were being additionally kind to me that morning, Tatiana included. A breath of shock escaped my lips when a plate landed in front of me at the dining room table, only for me to discover it was Tatiana who'd put it together for me. I looked down at it and nearly exploded. The breakfast eggs, hash browns, and bacon were all separated by rows of fruit; she'd remembered that I hate it when all my foods mixed together. I made the mistake of mentioning it to her, causing her to come back to shuffling everything together with a fork like she was a four year old, but I couldn't get mad at the little smirk that peeked out as she walked away, terribly amused with herself.

Cristiano lent me one of his suits to wear, as I'd awoken that morning realizing that I didn't have one. We finished breakfast and then went up to his room where he helped me put it on and tie the tie; all the fatherly things. It made me miss my own dad even more, which Cristiano identified and kept things light. My dad never got to teach me the ins and outs of suits. I'd opted out of junior prom given that I didn't have many friends or a date for that matter, and I expected to pretty much do the same with my senior prom, unless Harlie and I were still dating, which of course we weren't.

We stepped back from the mirror and Cristiano crisped the edges of the suit down. "There. Not bad for a teenager in an old man's threads."

I looked at myself in the mirror. The suit was simple and understated. It was a regular black with a thin black tie and a silver pin. We skipped the pocket square, as my hair hung down over the pocket anyway, and I wore my own black shoes, which I felt self-conscious of until Tatiana told me to quit moaning because if anyone was paying attention to my shoes, they were an asshole. In her own, trying not to cost herself her bitch-member-ship way, she was telling me it looked fine, and I accepted it.

She, on the other hand, looked heavenly, even for just going to attend a funeral. She was wearing a black dress that covered her shoulders, had one-quarter length sleeves, and flared at the bottom with a lace overlay. Her hair was up on top of her head in a ponytail, with her long, brown waves curling out and cascading down her back. She topped the ensemble off with a pair of black flats and just enough makeup to say she was wearing it; but Tatiana didn't need makeup, she had a kind of natural beauty that was amplified when she left her face untouched by fake products. I wouldn't tell her as much for fear of disrupting the stasis we'd found on the car ride, but I couldn't be more relieved that she was there. She was the only one who would be in that room that knew and loved my parents as much as I did. Most of the memories I had with them, she shared. It was like she was a link between the past and now, taking away some of the funeral's sinking finality, and replacing it with beautiful memories to live on forever.

Kya kept close to me as we loaded out of the car and headed for the church. Tons of people were already there, trying to file into the small chapel's single door. As I approached, someone noticed me, and they parted like the red sea to moses. I kept my head down as we moved between them. Inside, there were two large portraits of my parents with more flowers than I had ever seen in my life sitting in front of all the pulpits. My aunt was standing up next to them, greeting people as they walked in. It was almost painful how my aunt's blond hair and shining green eyes reminded me of my mom. They looked so much more alike than I realized.

"I should probably go up there, right?" I murmured.

Kya rubbed my back. "Only if you want to, sweetheart."

"I don't." I looked at her. "But I know that I should."

"I'll go with you." Cristiano tapped me on my back.

"I'm, uh, gonna go find a drinking fountain." Tatiana looked at me, as if asking for permission, but I nodded and she fluttered off.

"I'll be here." Kya side-stepped her way into one of the pews and sat down.

Cristiano brought me up to where my Aunt Hannah was standing. She smiled as soon as her eyes landed on me and she rushed towards me and pulled me into a huge hug. My eyes burned, threatening to reveal my emotions yet again, but I bit my lip to hold them back.

Hannah put her hand on my face. "Oh, hi honey. How are you feeling? How are things with the Marquettes?"

"They're being very good to me. I'm doing okay." I could quite determine if it was a lie or not. Was I doing okay? "How are you?"

"Well, getting all of this together so quickly wasn't fun, but it all came together."

I scratched my head. "Yeah. I'm sorry I didn't help much."

Hannah's eyes nearly plopped right out of her head. "Are you joking? I'm glad I was here to do it so you didn't have to. No child should have to do this." She put her hand on my arm. "I'm very sorry about all of this, sweetie."

"Thank you." I didn't know if it was habit or desperation that sent my head searching for Tatiana, but when I didn't see her, my anxiety doubled. "Uh. I'm going to go get something to drink."

"Want me to come?" both Hannah and Cristiano asked.

I held up my hands. "No. Really, I'll be okay."

I turned around to walk away from them and was met with an ocean of sympathetic faces. I tried to push through without acknowledging them, but every person I got within arm's reach of wanted to shake my hand or give me a hug or a pat of apology. They were hurling all manner of questions at me like what I planned to do with my parents' restaurant or if I was moving to New York? Was I inheriting my parents' house? Was I handing the restaurant over to the manager who worked there? Had my plan for after high-school changed?

Colin, what's next?

Colin, what's next?

Colin, what's next?

*I don't know.*

My plan to leave Colorado as soon as I was able, hopefully play football for a major university, and go pro was so far in the distance now, it was just a speck. I didn't know what the future held for me, all I knew was that I was suddenly faced with all of these important decisions that I wasn't ready to make. The pressure was breaking my bones.

I said a silent 'sorry' to my parents as I started to rudely force myself by people, just trying to get to the hallway. People were closing in on me like an iron maiden and I was being drained of life. I needed to breathe. I burst through the crowd and into the hallway. I let out a breath and nearly passed out from how long I'd been holding it. It felt 100 degrees cooler yet sweat was bleeding down my face in torrents.

"Are you okay?" I looked over and Tatiana was sitting against a wall, with her phone in her lap, looking up at me free of malice, but full of concern. She held up a bottle of water to me. "Here."

I walked over to where she was sitting and slid down against the wall opposite her. I sat and it felt like a two ton building was crashing off of me. I grabbed the bottle of water and took a huge gulp. "Thanks."

"Sorry I'm not in there."

"No, don't be. I don't want to be in there either." I tried to hand the bottle of water back, but she held out a hand telling me to keep it.

In the minutes that followed, Tatiana quietly flicked through her phone while I sat there staring at her. It should be a crime to be as beautiful as she was, and an even bigger one for me to still be so in love with her even after how she treated me. Maybe I was a sadist?

Tatiana looked up at me finally, I could only imagine she could feel my gaze drenching her. "So. How are you doing?"

I shrugged. "I'm okay."

She tilted her head to one side in disbelief. "Colin."

Hearing my name linger on her lips was the best sound I'd heard in years. "Yeah." She always could see right through me. "I'm overwhelmed. I keep getting all of these questions I don't know the answers to and I feel like everyone is expecting me to know what's next and I just… don't."

"Say that," she replied. "It's insensitive for people to throw all of this at you right now. Just tell them you don't know, that you're just trying to deal with today. They can accept it or they can f--" she looked around herself at the church, "fudge off."

I gave a quick smile at her correction before losing the grin again. "I don't know if I can do it."

"Well…" she sighs. "I can."

I furrowed my brow. "What?"

She got to her feet. "I can tell people to mind their own business. You just worry about staying on your feet." She held out a hand. "I'll go with you."

It was like someone had thrown a match on a bonfire they'd been covering in gasoline. Tatiana staring down at me, her hand outstretched, with a promise to be by my side, if only for a few hours, it lit a fire that blazed so high it was definitely going to burn me. I reached out and took her hand and let her pull me to my feet. Even once I was steady, I held on. Her skin was even softer than I remembered, warmer. She looked up at me, not pulling her hand back, and we stood there in a tense silence that could be split with a knife. I couldn't calculate it. The look in her eyes matched the way I felt, so why was there such dissonance between us? Why did she hurt me the way she did?

"I fucking knew it."

We looked over and Harlie was standing in the hallway to the church. More than a few students were in attendance, along with their parents, it only stood to reason that Harlie would be there too. She took one look at Tatiana and I holding hands and stormed out. I actually considered running after her, unsure of what she meant, but then I felt Tatiana pull my hand from hers and it dragged me back to attention.

She walked a few feet towards the door back into the chapel before looking over her shoulder at me. "You ready?"

If only that meant so much more than it did. "Yeah. I'm ready."

# 10

## TATIANA

I massaged the hand that Colin had hung onto with my other one. I thought about that day he kept hold of my hand at the mall and tried to push the feeling that it meant something more out of my mind. That was how I felt about that hand-hold too, but in the end, it didn't mean anything. Those moments between Colin and I always felt profound, like that single, rare second, the hour, minute, and second hands on a clock all line up. Blink and you miss it, but if you can be present in the moment, it feels like the earth itself stands to applaud.

But the second hand moves and that moment is gone. You blink wondering if it even happened at all or if you'd just made it up. Did you just make up his thumb gently smoothing across your skin or the 'I need you now' look in his eyes?

Probably.

"Good morning." I was wandering into the kitchen where my dad was mixing together a breakfast scramble, but I was far from home.

"Hey dad." I noticed neither my mom nor Colin was around. "Where is everyone?" My dad raised an eyebrow at me and my eyes flicked from side to side, searching for a reason for his piqued curiosity. "What?"

He shook his head. "Nothing." A light laugh bubbled out of him. "Colin had to meet with his lawyer, so your mother took him to deal with that this morning and then she's going to drop him off at school. Speaking of which," he pointed at the bar stool next to me where I noticed, for the first time, that Colin's backpack was sitting there. "I need you to bring his backpack to him."

"Come on dad," I whined, "we don't talk at school. Like at *all*. Everyone thinks I hate him." My dad's eyebrow went up again and it was starting to piss me off. "What?" I barked.

"So you're saying you *don't* hate him?"

Shit. I didn't even realize that I'd phrased my sentiments that way. "I mean… I… You know…

It's…" I shuddered and rolled my eyes. "I don't want to talk about it."

"Fine." My dad turned back to his pan and scooped some of the scramble onto a plate and slid it over to me. "Let's talk about something else then." I forked the eggs and threw them in my mouth, for some reason not anticipating how hot they'd be. "Careful, Tati!" My dad quickly fled to the fridge and poured me a glass of milk, handing it over, and I downed it. "Goodness. Anyway. Football is starting up this week, right?"

I looked up at him, this time my eyebrows were raised. "Uh, how the hell would I know?"

"I'm telling you it does." I shrugged and he rolled his eyes. "Colin is on the team. His parents went to all of his games so…"

I saw where the conversation was going and didn't like it. "No, dad. I'm not going to Colin's football games." I thought of how my younger self was waiting with bated breath for the opportunity. "I don't even like football."

"You used to. You liked the Broncos."

"I liked *horses*," I spat back. "Besides. There's no reason for me to be there."

"There is: the fact that I told you to be." He took my empty glass from me and refilled it.

"But dad, I--"

"No, Tatiana. You're going. I didn't want to say anything, because I know your mother has been pretty harsh with you, but the way you've responded towards Colin is beyond disappointing. We've all had to find ways to be cordial with people we don't care for, and I would think that given how close the two of you used to be and the fact that he lost *both* of his parents in a single night would have made you step up. I mean your mother and I raised you better than that. It's time for you to take whatever issues you two have and put them behind you. He's trying and I expect you to as well. We are going to his games as a family. End of discussion."

I groaned, but didn't respond. My dad wasn't the disciplinarian between my parents, and it wasn't often that he exerted any sort of parental dominance, but when he did, it was because the matter in question meant something to him. I was well aware of the way my parents were attempting to fill the void in Colin's life, I just didn't get why they were dragging me along for the ride. It killed me to spend so much time with Colin, why couldn't they see that?

My father and I didn't speak the entire rest of the morning. If my own emotions were going to be completely ignored while they were monkeying about trying to make Colin feel better, then I was better off not talking at all. My dad tried to toss some words of love and encouragement as I got out of the car, but I ignored them. I walked around the hood and started to head for the entrance when Ryan and Helena shot into my mind. What was the last thing Colin said to them?

I turned around and waved at my dad. "Love you, okay? Will you get out of here?"

He honked his dumb, should be broken Corola, and then drove away. I grinned as he left. I was lucky to have my parents, I knew that. That didn't change the fact that there were other factors at play. How was I supposed to balance all of it? I continued into the school with both mine and Colin's backpacks and started off towards his locker. I planned to just set it on the floor in front of it. Everyone knew his locker and his backpack and that his parents were brutally murdered. It would take a psychopath to steal it, and I didn't think there were any of them at Orchard Mesa high.

I got to the corner just before Colin's locker and heard a collection of voices, one of which belonged to Colin himself. Either the meeting had been fast or had been canceled for him to already be at school.

"I don't know, dude. I guess we all just kind of thought you did it because you were in mourning. You really aren't getting back together?"

I stopped shy of turning the corner.

"No," Colin responded, "we really aren't. She cheated on me. I saw it with my own eyes. I mean, the least she could have fucking done was waited until *after* my parents' funeral."

Harlie cheated on Colin and they broke up? What was all that at the funeral then? I thought she was mad thinking that *he* was cheating on *her?*

Another friend laughed. "I heard she thinks you were the one stepping out with Tatiana."

Colin scoffed. "Yeah, right. Do I look like a fucking masochist?"

It felt like a gut-punch. I'd been rough, there was no doubt about that, but I actually helped him get through his parents' funeral. Even after everything he did to me, I still supported him when he needed me. I looked at his backpack in my hand and felt like chucking it around the corner.

His friends were laughing. "Yeah, who the hell would go out with a bitch like that?"

I turned around and walked the other direction.

As some kid was passing by, I slammed the backpack in his chest with a gruff "Give this to Colin,"
and continued on without another thought. If they
took everything out of it, I wouldn't give a shit.

I made my way towards Val's office with my
blood pressure rising by the millisecond. *Who would
go out with me? Someone a lot fucking smarter than any of
you dipshits.*

I walked into Val's class, knowing he didn't have
a first period class, and shut the door behind me.

"Hey." His mouth was full of banana. He held
it up with a wicked smile. "Sorry, if I'd known you
were coming, I'd have brought two. Although," he
rolled his chair away from his desk so I could see his
crotch, "I'm sure we can find another one around
here."

I walked over to him and dropped to my knees
right in front of him. He flailed around, dropping
the banana on his desk and put his hands on my
shoulders. "Whoa, whoa, whoa. I was kidding."

"I'm not." I stared at him through a stone
serious expression.

"Look, as great an idea as I think it is to let you
near my dick with this visible rage you have going
on, I'm going to pass. Besides, I've got a few
colleagues headed in here any minute for a
meeting."

"Ugh!" I stood up and started to walk back towards the door.

"Whoa!" I heard his footsteps rushing behind me before I felt his hand grab my arm. "What's going on? What happened?"

I couldn't really tell him what had actually happened. I wasn't great at relationships, but I could only imagine telling your current boyfriend that you're livid because your former flame that you still have deep, unresolved feelings for insulted you, probably doesn't make for a long, happy life.

"My dad is making me go to Colin's games with him." I was grateful for something adjacent that made me almost as frustrated.

"Ah." He pulled me back towards his desk and sat me down in his chair. He crouched in front of me and rested his arms on my lap and his head on top of those. "And you're pissed because you can't stand him now and don't want to show him any more support than you have to?"

I shrugged, not really wanting to talk about this with Val either. "I guess. I don't know. I don't even like football."

"Yeah, that's because you're intelligent," Val replied and I could feel football fans' around the nation's spidey senses going off that someone had insulted them. I also didn't agree, but it worked better for my current circumstances if I did, so I kept my mouth shut. "So you'll be at the game on Wednesday night?"

"Yeah." I remembered suddenly that I was supposed to 'spend the night at Billy's' on Wednesday so that I could be with Val. "Oh. Sorry, we'll probably have to switch nights."

"Maybe not." His fingers walked across my thigh, inching further and further up. "I'll go to the game too. We can sneak under the bleachers."

I snickered. "Are you serious?"

Val's amused smile when straight-laced in an instant. "Dead." He grinned again. "Our bleachers are tarped in the back. Unless anyone has the same idea, we'll be safe."

"And if someone has the same idea?" I asked.

"Then we pretend I'm giving you CPR. It's fool-proof."

My mood was lightening a bit. "I don't quite see it that way."

"Come on." He poked at me. "You were the one who said you wanted a little risk."

I thought about it for a second, imagining the thrill. It might help to jump start the listlessness I'd settled into since Colin moved in. "Okay. I'm in."

I told Billy about Val's and my plan at lunch, and staunchly avoided making any form of eye-contact with Colin despite the number of times he looked at me. We didn't share any classes as students from two different years, so lunch was our only communal time of the day. Ordinarily, I'd be going out of my way to at least flip him off, but his words were etched across my brain and I avoided him to keep from starting an all-out war. I was stupid for even entertaining the idea that things were shifting between us. He was still the same reel-her-in-then-let-her-go asshole he'd always been.

I'd planned to head home without him after school, but he'd gotten outside before me. I kept my headphones in my ear, my backpack over my shoulder, and just kept walking when he looked up at me with an innocent smile. I know better now, Undinger. Fuck that smile.

I could see him out of the corner of my eye, shuffling to keep up with my quick strides, and eventually, I felt him pull on my arm. I yanked it away from him and continued, but he grabbed me again.

I snatched my headphone out of my left ear and glared at him. "What do you want?"

"What's wrong? Did something happen at school?" he asked and his naive expression pissed me off.

"Yeah, apparently I'm a sadist."

Colin looked as if I'd just slapped him in the face. "Oh…"

I put my headphone back in and started to walk again, but Colin grabbed my arm once again. I tried to pull away, but he grabbed my headphone and pulled it out of my ear and held it above his head. Colin was over 6 feet and I was lucky to be allowed on rides at the amusement park.

"Give that back." My tone was low and seething.

"Just let me talk." I didn't really have a choice. I crossed my arms and he brought his arm down a little, but not so close I could grab my gadget. "I didn't mean that."

I blinked a couple of times, the anger leaving me like a deflating balloon. "What?"

"I just said that, because I'm hurting? Because I'm stupid? I don't know." He furrowed his brow. "But you have been acting kind of sadistic lately, just FYI."

And just like that he patched the balloon. What was left of my rage had my hand flying at his stomach. I didn't make contact, but when he doubled over to try and dodge it, his hand came down enough that I could grab my headphone. I took it, put it back in my ear and started off with him calling after me.

People can't just say horrible things because they're hurting.

*'Gross. I would never be his girlfriend.'*

*Shut up, brain. That was then, this is now.*

## 11

## COLIN

"Undinger, you good? I thought you'd be elated for the first game?"

I was sitting on the bench in the locker room lost in thought when my football coach, Damian Nash, walked up to me. The rest of the guys were all floating around, buzzing with excitement as the first game of our season got closer to beginning, but I was distracted. I had everything on my mind from my parents to Tatiana, and mostly I just wanted to go home and crawl into bed.

Coach Nash sat down next to me on the bench and I felt immediately calmed by his presence. He was the kind of guy that you could trust with your grandma, but also could hide behind if someone suddenly appeared with a gun. He had deep brown skin, but glowing hazel eyes, and brown hair that was dreaded and flowed down his back. He had a muscular upper build, which made him feel larger than he was, given he was actually rather slim and was just under six feet tall. He was our high school's student counselor by day and our varsity football coach by night. There wasn't a student in the school that didn't like him.

"Hey, coach. Um, I guess I'm just a little lost in thought."

That was an understatement. I was thinking about Tatiana and how she could honestly be surprised that I would call her sadistic. She seemed to take pleasure out of torturing me, and had even admitted herself that she went too far sometimes. She'd flipped on a dime back when we were kids and had been downright evil to me ever since. Sure, a few of our recent interactions made me think that maybe there was something hidden deep, deep, *deep* beneath her surface that still held something for me, but the fact that I had to claw through miles of thorny bushes to get to it almost didn't feel worth it. I loved her, probably more than I had loved anything in my life, but was I prepared to sacrifice that much of my sanity? How much of myself would I lose trying to find her?

Then there was Harlie. It was a shock to say the

least that she thought I was sleeping around on her when we'd had multiple conversations about my former flame. It was even more surprising that she thought it was Tatiana, when I'd been very careful to only tell her I had been in love before, but never with who. I'd told her time and again how much infidelity hurt me, and knowing Harlie as a person, she probably went that route just to spite me. It was a big misunderstanding, based on what I didn't know, but a misunderstanding nonetheless. Did I see myself marrying Harlie someday? No. But was she something like a friend when I had very few to speak of? Yes. I couldn't decide if I wanted to clear the air and make nice with her, even if it meant 'getting back together.' The thought of being anything other than single at that point made my skin crawl, but I might have found myself in a 'lesser of two evils' situation: but who was the lesser of two evils?

"Well, you know," Coach Nash pierced my thoughts with his NPR-esque voice. "I'm always here to talk if you need me, but I need you in top form tonight. Game one. We've got a reputation to set."

"I'm on it coach." I stood up from the bench. "Let's go get this win."

Coach Nash stood up and punched my chest. "That's what I'm talking about! Let's do it!"

Coach Nash gathered the team and led us in his inspirational, beginning of the season speech. For about half the team, it was the final season of their high school careers. I fell into that category, and the more Coach Nash talked, the more pumped up I got. I didn't want to tank the first game of my final season because I was thinking of two women, both of whom had shown me that they couldn't really give a rat's ass about my emotions. The sadness in me started to seep out of me as anger started to seep in. What the hell was I doing letting those two occupy so much of my brain?

"Bring it in, boys! Tigers on three!" Coach Nash put his hand in the middle of the huddle and everyone piled theirs on top of his. "One, two, three."

"TIGERS!"

The team broke and everyone rushed out of the locker rooms and out onto the field. There was a roar of fans as we ran out. A vast majority of the Orchard Mesa community was packed into those bleachers. They all wore different shades of orange and black and cheered on the players they knew as we ran over to our bench. I scanned the crowd even though I knew I wouldn't see my parents' warm, inviting faces among it. I would never see their faces again.

A shudder ran down my spine. It was an unexpected experience. I was working on coming to terms with the fact that they were gone in general, but I hadn't considered moments like these. All the 'firsts.' The first time they weren't there to say goodbye to me when I went to school in the morning, the first time they weren't there to greet me when I got home--the first time they weren't there to cheer me on at football. My throat collapsed in on itself and I felt like I couldn't breathe. Even with the cool night air slicing against my face, I was burning up.

"Undinger." Coach Nash was at my side in a second. I blinked and all of my teammates who'd been behind me a second ago, were suddenly all the way over at the bench already. How did they move so fast? "You good? You just sort of froze."

"Um…" I took a deep breath, trying to bury my pain. "Yeah. I'm good."

"Check that out."

Coach Nash pointed towards the sea of people and followed his finger to a few people situated on the bottom most bleacher, dressed head to toe in the school colors, and waving at me wildly. It was Kya and Cristiano Marquette, and next to them was Tatiana. She was dressed in black as she normally was, but she did have an orange scarf wrapped around her neck. When my eyes landed on her, she grinned a little before flipping me a middle finger. It wasn't the malicious way she'd done it in the past, but more like she was letting me know, in her own way, that she was there.

I took another deep breath, feeling the life that had been attempting to untether itself from my body, settle back in.

"Let's give 'em a show, eh?" Coach Nash tapped my back and started to push me over towards the bench.

The crowd slowly started to chant my name, pushing as much of their energy into me as I could muster. Even though it was like they were just getting me to half-battery, I was hoping it would be enough to get me through the game without making a total fool of myself.

I was wrong.

The first half was coming to a close in the blink of an eye. We were down 6-13, and all eyes were on me to get the ball downfield in the hopes of snagging a touchdown. I knew my runners could get down there, and my linemen had me covered, but I was punctured by the lack of my parents. It was as if I'd forgotten how to throw a football. The snap happened, and then the ball was in my hands. I backed down the field under the roar of the fans cheering me on, but my teammates bolting down the turn were just a blend of colors to me. I wanted to get the ball out to one of them, but no one looked open. A tackle broke through the line and charged right at me, ramming into me hard and sweeping me clear off my feet. It was the second sack I'd taken that game, but this time, when I smashed against the ground, the ball went slipping out of my hands like a greased up melon. The other team's wide-receiver leapt over me and scooped up the ball before I could get back to it, racing at top speed for his end-zone.

"TOUCHDOWN!"

The entire ocean of black and orange-clad fans groaned with defeat while the opposing team cheered. One of my teammates helped me to my feet, but I could see in his eyes that he was pissed.

"Carter was wide open." He dropped my hand and started for the bench as the announcer signified the end of the first half.

I trudged over to the rest of the team and started to file back into the locker room. They all kept a wide distance from me like I was covered in some disease. I couldn't blame them. If I were in their position and the first game of my senior year was going the way it was because of me, I'd stay away from me too.

Coach Nash grabbed my shoulder and held me back from the group, already getting water and hissing insults. "Two sacks, Undinger. That's tough."

"I'm sorry coach. I'll do better in the second half, I promise," I replied.

Coach Nash shook his head. "Colin, I'm sorry. I can see that you're just not in the right place, and I'm afraid you're gonna get hurt. I can't put you back out there."

My jaw fell slack. "What? No. Coach. I promise. I'm good. Please, just let me--"

"I'm sorry, Colin. I couldn't call myself a coach, counselor, or friend if I let you go back out there like this. They'll take your head off." He noogied my head. "Don't worry. You'll be back to your old self in no time. There's still plenty of season left." He walked away without letting me offer any additional protests and I was very tempted to pull off my pads and storm out of there without another word. If it weren't for the coach's 'We support even when we can't play,' rule I probably would have.

So in the second half I was sitting on the bench like a chump. The team was getting ready for the second half to start, with the newest quarterback to the team, some Sophomore hopeful, was getting caught up on plays. Each time I looked over at Kya and Cristiano, they were giving me thumbs up and cheering for me despite the fact that it was clear I'd been benched. I smiled back at them, but it made me feel lame. I wanted to repay their support with an impressive game, not by getting my back blown out.

I looked over at Tatiana, but she was buried in her phone. Any friendly glance from her might have been enough to make me feel less shitty, but I watched as she continued to ignore me, and everything, all up until her head shot up and she started looking around the field. A little bit of confidence bled into me letting me think she was looking for me somewhere on the field, but then her eyes landed on someone standing off to the side of the bleachers near the concession stand.

I continued to watch her curiously, mentioning something to her parents, and then eventually standing up off the bleachers. She walked down to the stairs and over to a figure in a dark gray hoodie and jeans. At first I thought it may have been a visiting student, but Tatiana reached up and pulled the hood back, and though he was still hard to make out, his long hair was famous around our school; it was Mr. Kepler, one of the science teachers. Tatiana was standing closer to him than what I thought was normal for a teacher and student, but that was nothing compared to the fact that, after looking around them to make sure no one was watching them, Mr. Kepler took Tatiana's hand and led her behind the bleachers.

My head frantically looked all around me, wondering if anyone was seeing what I was seeing, but everyone was watching the game. My eyes kept flicking to the game clock, but not to see how much time was left in the game, but to clock how long Mr. Kepler and Tatiana were behind the bleachers. Three minutes passed, five minutes passed, ten, eleven, twelve, twelve and one half, twelve and three quarters, thirteen...

Twenty minutes passed before Mr. Kepler re-emerged from behind the bleachers. I felt like I was going to be sick as I watched them smoothing their clothes down and fixing their hair. Mr. Kepler wrapped his arm around Tatiana's back, but she pushed him off, brushing a hand through his hair before starting away from him. As she was walking away, he swiped a hand out and swatted her on her ass. I watched her for signs of disgust or fear, but the only one who felt those things was me as Tatiana giggled and waved goodbye to Mr. Kepler, who pulled his hood up and made for the exit.

"Holy crap," I whispered out loud.

*Tatiana is sleeping with Mr. Kepler.*

## 12

## COLIN

For the first night since my parents died, the reason I couldn't bring myself to sleep was due to something other than their passing. Every time I closed my eyes, I saw Tatiana's smile aimed at Mr. Kepler and his hand reaching out to smack her ass. There was no questioning what I'd witnessed. I didn't have to see them doing anything to know that when they'd slid behind the bleachers, it was to have sex. That was the kind of thing that was disturbing enough when two teenagers did it, let alone a teenager and a teacher. I was hopelessly torn between whether I was more troubled by learning that Tatiana was seeing someone in general or the fact that that person was one of our high school teachers. Maybe I was way off base with calling her a sadist. If she was sneaking around with one of the teachers at school, she was probably closer to being a masochist.

Around one o'clock in the morning, when I thought I was going to successfully manage to go to sleep without thinking about Tatiana's toxic affair, it hit me that three days a week she stayed after school for tutoring. Tatiana was one of the most intelligent people I'd ever met, and I knew just from seeing her around that almost all of her classes were advanced placement or a year up from where she was. She didn't need tutoring. She was staying after school, three days a week, to have sex with the science teacher.

That really fucked me up.

All I wanted to do was pick up my phone and call my mom. She was one of the most reasonable and understanding people on the planet, paired with the fact that up until her dying day, she loved Tatiana like a daughter. She was always giving me the play-by-play on Tatiana's life that she'd gotten in her daily reports from Kya. She regularly asked me to talk to her at school. The day Tatiana broke my heart, I cried in my mom's arms for close to two hours. She tried to coax me into talking to her to try and get to the bottom of what happened, but whenever I tried to talk to Tatiana, she ignored me.

Eventually I just lost the steam to continue to chase after her. I was certain my mom had tried a time or two to force the conversation by inviting the Marquettes to a free dinner at the restaurant, but every time she did, Kya and Cristiano would show up without Tatiana in tow.

I would have told my mom everything if she was still around to tell it to. I didn't keep secrets from my parents; I didn't need to. I wished I could have asked my mom for advice about the weird, intimate looks Tatiana and I had shared a few times, or what to do now that she was actually tolerating being in the same room as me. I'd ask her what I should do now that I know Tatiana is seeing a teacher. She'd have the perfect answer too, she always had the perfect answer.

The morning was awkward for me. It was like everything she did was tainted with an odd color, like a TV that somehow ended up on the wrong visual setting. It was just Tatiana enjoying cereal for breakfast, it was Tatiana, who was sleeping with a teacher, enjoying cereal. It wasn't just Tatiana prattling on with her dad on the car ride to school, it was Tatiana, who was sleeping with a teacher, prattling on. What would her parents say if they knew? I could only imagine they'd be as horrified as I was, probably worse.

"What?" Tatiana snapped at me finally as we were walking into school.

"What?" I replied.

She rolled her eyes. "You've been staring at me with this weird look all morning. Is there something you want to say or are you afraid of telling a sadist like me?" I opened my mouth to respond, but she broke and started laughing. "I'm kidding. About the sadist thing, I mean, not about the weird look. Is there something I should know?"

Having Tatiana smile at me was always wonderful. Whether by choice, or by heavy-handed coaxing from her parents, she appeared to be letting the sadist thing go. I suppose I could take that win at least.

"I don't know what you mean," I lied.

Tatiana scoffed. "Well, that's a complete lie." I might have expected that she, of all people, would be able to read me like a children's picture book. "But, I suppose I'm not in any position to force you to tell me the truth." *Sure you are.* She flipped me the bird. "Bye."

She turned the corner to walk away from me once we were inside the doorframe, and I suddenly felt compelled to say something. "Uh, Tati." She turned and looked back at me, eyes wide. I was confused at first, but then realized I used her nickname for the first time since we'd parted ways the day I kissed her. "Ana," I added quickly. "Tatiana. I have a question for you."

She stood about ten feet from me with her arms crossed. "Okay?"

I didn't know what to do. I'd acted on compulsion to call her name, but I couldn't rightfully ask her in the middle of the school hallway about her relationship with a teacher. "Um." I thought about it as deeply as I could, but no answer came to me. I couldn't talk to her about it now, so now I had to figure out what to say. "Did you talk to Harlie recently?"

*Shit. Colin. This is not a good alternate route.*

Tatiana's jaw tensed a little bit. "I mean… I talked to her the day after… you know."

I fled from one corner and walked right into another one. "Did you say anything about… us."

"Us?" Tatiana replied, an honest height to her voice, like she truly had no idea what I was talking about. Had I really messed everything up by kissing her back then? If I'd have known it was going to cost me our friendship, I never would have done it.

"You know what? Nevermind." It was dumb starting this conversation right now. Any information I wanted about what happened between

Tatiana and Harlie was going to have to come from Harlie. "See ya."

I turned around without waiting for her response and started off. I felt like an idiot. Not only had I not gotten anywhere with trying to find out about Tatiana and Mr. Kepler, I'd opened a can of worms about our pasts that was probably going to bite me in the ass later. I passed my locker entirely, and walked up to Harlie, who was chatting absent-mindedly with her friends. As soon as I approached, her friends scattered like roaches when the light turned on. I must have been their topic of conversation.

Harlie turned her back to me and started sifting through her locker, even though I could see she wasn't looking for anything specific. "Colin."

"Can I talk to you?" I didn't have time for fake pleasantries. "Somewhere private? There's been a misunderstanding."

Harlie looked over her shoulder at me briefly before grabbing something out of her locker and then slamming it shut. "Fine. Let's go to the courtyard."

I followed Harlie down the hallway, trying my best to ignore the points and whispers that found us as we walked. Our school was full of gossips. Harlie pushed her way through the door that led out to the high school courtyard. Our school was essentially a giant square, with a majority of each grade's classes being situated in a different wing, along the edges of the square, with all of the electives and extracurricular classes being situated in the middle. In the bullseye of the square was a small courtyard with the greenery the gardening club maintained, and a statue of our founder. Students who needed fresh air were allowed to go out into the courtyard throughout the day, though it was mostly empty in the mornings on a fall day due to the chilly weather.

Harlie made her way over to one of the benches and sat down, crossing one leg over the other, and staring at me as though she'd already started an 'explanation countdown timer' in her head. Her attitude kind of pissed me off. *She* was the one who cheated on *me*.

I walked up to where she was and stayed standing in front of her. "First of all, can you drop this?" I asked motioning to her. "You kissed someone else, not me."

"Really?" Harlie asked. "You haven't kissed anyone else?"

"No." The conviction in my voice was as solid as stone. "I've only kissed one person besides you and it was five years ago."

Harlie uncrossed her legs and relaxed her shoulders. "Are you being serious?"

"Yeah. I've told you a thousand times that I take loyalty in relationships very seriously. I don't know what you heard, but I wasn't seeing anyone but you. I'm still not."

Harlie swallowed hard as her mistake washed over her. "That's not what it looked like on Saturday."

"Yeah." I sat down next to her. "Tatiana's parents and my parents were really close, so we were good friends as a kid. I was feeling over-whelmed and she was helping me out. That was it."

"You didn't kiss?"

"No. It was just shitty timing. The only reason we were holding hands is because she had *just* helped me stand up." I thought of the way I held Tatiana's hand in mine and the way she looked at me when I did. It was hard to think that I was just confusing her feelings.

"Wow." Harlie buried her hands between her legs and looked to the ground. "I'm sorry, Colin. I just wanted to hurt you the way you hurt me. I don't even care about that guy. I took a selfie of us and I was going to post it, I didn't expect you to find out before that."

"I came over to your house to talk and saw it," I explained.

She looked up at me, and for as nasty of a person as I'd seen her be, she looked genuinely sad. "I'm so sorry. Some girlfriend I am. You lose your parents and I thank you by kissing someone else." Her hand slid over and rested on my leg. "Is there any chance that we could…"

"I don't know." I didn't put my hand on top of hers. "I forgive you, I understand it was just a mixup, but doing that instead of talking to me? I just don't know if I can let that go. I need time to think about it."

Harlie pulled her hand back. "I understand. I'll give you all the space you need. For what it's worth, I really *am* sorry."

"I know." I offered her a small smile. "I can see it."

She smiled back at me. "Good. Still friends at least?"

I nodded. "At least." That seemed to give her some hope. "Listen. Can I ask your advice on something? I saw some really crazy shit yesterday and I don't really have anyone else to talk to about it."

"Sure." She crossed her legs again, this time to lean in with curiosity. "What's up?"

I didn't want to be *totally* honest. Harlie and Tatiana didn't get along and I didn't want to stoke that flame. "I think a friend of mine might be sleeping with one of her teachers."

Harlie's eyes widened. "Are you serious? That's wild. What makes you think that?"

I was trying to circumvent enough details that she couldn't guess the participants. "I saw it. Not like the sex, but the before and after. It was obvious." Harlie looked up to the sky and I could see her calculating, it made me instantly nervous. I'd been very vague, she couldn't have figured it out based on the few details I provided. "What?"

"You thought we were good until Friday right before your parents' funeral and if it had happened earlier in the week, I assume you would have come to me sooner. So this happened at the game last night, which means it's probably a teacher and student from this school."

Damn she was good. "Uh, no, I…"

"And you don't have many friends, no offense, definitely no other girls but me, but you said 'her' when you first said it." Fuck. Her eyes got wide all of a sudden and her head turned back to me. "Is it Tatiana Marquette?" Fuck times two. "Oh my god. It is! Holy shit! She's sleeping with one of the teachers? Which one?"

I shook my head. It was a bad idea to go to Harlie. "N-n-no. You've got is wr--"

Harlie let out a huge gasp and stood up off the fountain. "Oh my god! The day after your parents passed I heard a rumor that Mr. Kepler kicked students out of his classroom twice to talk to her! It's Mr. Kepler! Tatiana Marquette is sleeping with Mr. Kepler! Holy crap! This is crazy!"

"Shhh." I grabbed her hand and pulled her down to sit again. "I shouldn't have even said anything. You can't tell anyone."

Harlie was shaking her head wildly. "I won't."

"Harlie, swear to god you won't say anything?"

"I won't, I won't, I won't." Her eyes were glowing with excitement. I wasn't counting on her not sharing the juicy news I'd just given her about one of her mortal enemies. "Wow," she huffed. "Well, I guess that's a solid notch. Mr. Kepler is hot."

That was the last thing I wanted to hear. "You promise you aren't going to say anything?"

Harlie took her right pointer finger and drew an 'X' across her chest, and then stuck her hand in the air. "Cross my heart, Colin. Your secret is safe with me."

## 13

## TATIANA

Things were starting to reach a level of 'normalcy' as my parents and I started getting used to having Colin around; as used to it as we could. My parents were fine. In their mind, they just had two kids now, and they had to make up for years of not having one of them by being overly kind and generous to him. For me, it was totally different. It wasn't just like having an old friend around, hell a total stranger might have been better. It was Colin, and being around Colin was doing things to me that I neither anticipated nor was equipped to handle. Dealing with him was like trying to turn a burner on to the perfect setting. I was either getting it too hot or too cold; too mean, or holding his hand and staring into his beautiful green eyes as though nothing bad had ever happened between us.

There had to be a happy medium.

Both my parents had made their displeasure with my response to Colin known. I had explained it to my mom well enough, and I could feel her laying off the 'forced family' bit a little, but not enough to let me fade back into the obscure parts of his mind like I was hoping. As I laid in bed, with the Saturday morning sun tickling my caramel skin, I was beginning to think that the best way to get through suddenly living with Colin unscathed was to try and get back to the friendly place we'd once been in. I didn't know how well I'd do being friends with Colin, especially when my repressed feelings were clawing at the lid of the cage I'd locked them in, but if things could be cordial between us, enjoyable even, wasn't that the way to go? My parents would be happy, Colin would be happy (I hoped), and I would be... well... I could survive it.

I grabbed my laptop from my bedside table and sat up enough to rest it in my lap. Orchard Mesa was kind of a kitsch place. It was where people came when they wanted to be in Colorado without being 'typical' and as a result, there was always something going on. Outdoor concerts, random competitions, model-boat racing; if it was just off the radar enough to not seem touristy, but could still gather a crowd, it was easy to find in O.M.

I sifted through the online versions of different local papers until I came across something that seemed interesting enough. 'A Trip Around the World Food Festival.' That was safe enough. It didn't suggest that I was up to anything or making any sort of lurid suggestion. That's where two friends go on a Saturday, a food festival.

I hopped out of bed and started for my door, just barely catching the look of myself in my floor-length mirror as I passed it. I backed up until I could observe myself honestly. Dark gray pajama pants that hung past my feet, a black tank-top, and hair that screamed 'I just woke up.' That wasn't going to do. I skipped over to my closet and started to throw clothes around looking for something to wear. At first, I pulled out jeans and a hoodie, but that looked a little too done up for emerging from my room for the first time. I looked over my PJs again. Maybe I *should* just go casual.

"Ugh!" I growled out loud to myself. What the hell was I doing? Was I seriously trying to decide what to wear to leave my goddamn bedroom?

"No." I threw down the jeans and hoodie and walked back over to my door.

I grabbed the doorknob and hesitated. I was still braless. I didn't have the biggest bust around, but I was still sporting a healthy 34-C. Enough to bounce when I moved at the very least. If I walked over to Colin's bedroom with them throwing a dance party, that probably *would* seem suggestive. I walked back to the closet, scooped up the hoodie, pulled it over, and walked out before I could talk myself out of it.

I crossed the hallway to where Colin was staying and stood outside his door. Why couldn't I bring myself to knock on it? I wasn't asking him to prom or anything, just to a food festival. I lifted my hand to knock and froze.

Should I go back for the jeans?

The door opened and Colin appeared. He jumped at the sight of me, and so did I. "Fuck!"

*Well done, Tatiana.* "God. I'm sorry."

"What are you doing?" Colin was clutching his head. He was wearing just a pair of basketball shorts and a tank top, with hair that screamed 'I just woke up.' Somehow I felt like I lost a battle, especially because despite his dressed down appearance, he was mind-numbingly gorgeous. "Are you okay?"

"Yes!" I realized I'd been quiet for way too long, just staring at him. "I was wondering what you were up to today?"

Colin cocked his head to the side and my heart did a tiny cheer. It was so cute. "What?"

"What?" I asked.

"Why do you want to know what I'm up to today?"

I bunched my brow. "I can't ask?"

"You can. It's just unexpected." Colin crossed his arms. "I don't really have any plans for today."

"Well…" I took a breath. "There's this food festival today. It's called A Trip Around the World, or something. Do you… Uh, would you like to go?"

"With you?" Colin's eyes got wider.

My blood was pumping so fast I could hear it in rhythmic thrums in the back of my ears. "I mean, I'd also be there."

Colin smiled and it was like a knockout punch. "I'd love to."

"Okay. Well. These things are always better earlier in the day versus later. Could you be ready to go in like thirty minutes?" I asked.

Colin's grin got even bigger. "I'll be ready in fifteen."

God damn it. All I needed was for him to be a little less… *him*. A little less like a warm blanket on a cold day. A little less like the first flowers in spring. Just... a little less.

"I'll be ready in thirty," I hissed back, trying to keep my demeanor even, but Colin chuckled in response. "Meet you downstairs."

I returned to my room before I could say or do anything stupid, and had to take a minute to gather myself. I pushed all the thoughts, both sweet and spicy, flooding my brain and went for the jeans I'd picked out earlier. I picked out a different hoodie, a dark green one that I hadn't worn in a long time, and put my hair up in a ponytail. I grabbed a pair of comfy tennis-shoes for walking for a long time and opened my bedroom door to head back out.

As I walked out, Colin emerged from his room as well, wearing a pair of tan cargo shorts, a black zip-up sweatshirt, and had his hair hanging loose under a black baseball cap.

Have mercy.

If I had three wishes, I would use all of them to wish that Colin was just a tiny bit uglier. He smirked. "You beat me." Then again, maybe I wouldn't.

He allowed me to lead down the stairs. By my parents' expressions, you could have thought we walked in stark naked. My mom looked like she was going to spit out her coffee.

"Good morning," she greeted.

"Hi," we replied in unison and then exchanged an amused glance.

My dad started to smile. "I didn't expect you two to be awake so early, and here in the kitchen, at the same time… and so close." I took a large step to my left, putting some distance between Colin and I, and glared at my dad. "Sorry."

"What's up?" My mom asked.

I sat down at one of the barstools and Colin sat down next to me, making my body heat up exponentially. "Uh, there's this food festival downtown today. I was wondering if we could take one of the cars."

My mom stood up and went to stand by my dad with a silly, amused grin on. "Together? You're going together?"

I rolled my eyes so hard I thought I was going to sprain them. "Yeah, mom. We're going together!"

"Sorry!" My mom side-eyed my dad and I wanted to murder them both. "Of course. Take my car. No use risking your dad's."

"Hey. My Corolla is solid."

"Yeah, a solid piece of crap." Colin giggled at my mom's joke and it caused me to laugh as well. It was such a joyous, contagious sound. She reached on top of the fridge and grabbed her purse. She dived into it and pulled out her keys and handed them over, then she opened her wallet. "How much do you think will do it for the day? $200?"

I was shocked and I could see Colin's jaw drop out of the corner of my eye. "Um, $200 would definitely cover it."

My mom nodded and then pulled a small handful of bills out of her hands. She often carried cash. As a personal consultant for people's small businesses, they often paid her in cash. She'd make every other day trips to the bank so she never had too much on her at one time. She counted out $200 in $20s and handed them over to me. I started to fold the bills to put them in my own wallet when I noticed her start to flick through the bills again. I watched in amazement as she counted out an additional $200 in $20s and handed the cash to Colin.

Colin reached out wearily. "You don't have to do this."

"Are you kidding?" My mom snapped her wallet closed and returned it to her purse. "I'm so happy you two are going out to do something together that you had room to negotiate. I got off easy for what I would have paid."

I shook my head at her. "You are the weirdest."

"Do you need breakfast or will you eat there?" my dad asked.

Colin looked at me and in a split second, I knew we were on the same page. He looked back at my dad. "I think we're safer going in with empty stomachs."

I nodded in agreement and my dad clapped his hands. "Alright. Have fun then, you two."

I stood up and Colin followed suit. We said our final goodbyes and went out to my mom's Chevy Equinox. It made my dad's car look like an antique. Colin looked at it and laughed as he climbed into the passenger's seat.

"I can't believe your dad still has that car."

I started up the engine. "It's really astounding that the wheels haven't fallen off. It doesn't track miles anymore. It maxed out."

Colin laughed. "I didn't even know cars did that."

"Me either."

The car ride was a ping-ponging of awkward silence and both Colin and I's attempts to start conversations just to break that silence. It felt like a huge relief when we were finally getting out of the car at the downtown event space where the festival was being held, but then we had to navigate walking next to each other. How close was too close? How far was too far? When we got to the ticket counter, we both sort of hesitated as we approached. Do we buy tickets together? Separate? It was exhausting to navigate. Finally, Colin stepped up to the ticket counter and purchased two tickets. I was standing several feet behind him when he stepped up, expecting him to just get one, so when he said two, I took a giant step towards him to not seem even *more* awkward, a mission I failed when he turned and we collided.

Colin reached out and grabbed my arm to keep me from toppling over and I wanted to die. Why was it so hard? We used to hang out all the time and it was never that bad, and I was in love with him then too.

"You good?" Colin asked, his hand still gripped around my arm.

"Yeah, sorry." He released me and then handed over the second ticket. I took it, wanting terribly to turn back time. "Thanks."

"Yeah." There was a slight chuckle to his voice.

We passed through the security checkpoint, showed our tickets, and entered the festival. The typically divided event center had been opened up so it was one huge, open space. Different booths formed a colorful maze that was oozing with a variety of delicious smells. The purpose of the festival was food, of course, but there were several entertainment and merchandise stalls set up in each 'country.' With the throngs of people feeding in and out of each divided row were enough to make the added effort worth it. Plenty more than food would be sold at the festival that day, and with my mom's money burning a hole in each of our pockets, Colin and I would be contributing.

We walked the first row of stalls in silence. Our space issue was solved, as the number of people around us forced us to walk shoulder to shoulder, but it only made the awkwardness worse. We were so close that we were uncomfortable, so neither of us disrupted the little bit of stasis we had struck by saying anything. My stomach was growling amidst all the delicious food, but I was almost too afraid to say anything. I was trying to work up the gumption to admit I was hungry, when I felt a hand grab mine. I looked down and saw that Colin had grabbed me. I looked up at him, not certain what I would see, but noticed him staring off to the right with a shocked expression.

He pointed out with his free hand. "Oh my god, Tati, look."

My skin prickled at the sound of my nickname skating across his lips. I followed his finger to where he was pointing. "What?" My eyes found what he was looking at. Standing in front of the France pavilion, was a massive Dr. Louis Pawscal mascot; a character from a show that Colin and I religiously watched as kids. He was a doberman pinscher with a stethoscope hanging around his neck and a white, doctor's coat over his back. "Is Dr. Pawscal still a thing?"

It was a France-based cartoon that was recorded only in french. When we were little kids, we discovered it by accident and fell in love with Dr. Pawscal's crazy adventures trying to be a dog doctor in a human world, even though we never had any idea what he was saying. We would sit in his living room for hours, making up our own dialogue to the show until it was finally adapted to an English version, which we enjoyed less.

Colin whipped his head towards me. "We have to go and take a picture."

I laughed. "We are seventeen years old." Colin was a few months older than me. He'd have his eighteenth birthday in a few weeks, but mine wasn't until after the holidays.

"So! Look at him!" I looked over and it did look kind of sad. No kids were interacting with him, and those parents who knew who he was and were trying to force their children over, were being met with severe resistance. "He needs some fun!"

Suddenly, Colin was that little boy I knew all those years ago. "Okay." I smiled. "Let's go."

"Yes!" Colin dragged me through the crowd until we were over to Dr. Pawscal. "Hey! Dr. Pawscal!"

The mascot jumped up, and even though he was stuck with the painted on smile, we could tell our excitement had given him new energy.

I pulled out my phone. "Can we have some selfies?"

Dr. Pawscal jumped and down and waddled over and we rushed over to him. We spent the next five minutes taking a variety of selfies. We'd almost lost steam at the two minute mark, but then Dr. Pawscal revealed that his stethoscope could be pulled off, so we of course needed shots with each of us wearing *it* as well. To our delight, our enjoyment turned into a twister that sucked in several of the families around us, and before too long, a line was forming, all of the kids excitedly waiting to take their own pictures with Dr. Pawscal.

Colin and I dragged our damn near adult selves away so that the kids could start to hang out with Dr. Pawscal, and we smiled as we stood off to the side, watching all the kids yelp and cheer.

Colin started to flip through the pictures he'd

taken with his phone with a broad smile on his face. "That was awesome."

It was. There was one picture in particular on my phone that had Dr. Pawscal holding his stethoscope up to Colin's chest like he was testing his pulse, and I had the back of my hand to Colin's head like he had a fever. Colin had a blinding smile on his face. I would keep that picture forever.

"Alright, food?" Colin asked.

My stomach growled to remind me that it was, in fact, hungry. "Please."

"Let's go this way. There was a lavender tea stand in Japan." He started off, but I didn't immediately move. I loved lavender tea. He remembered. "Tati?" he asked when he saw that I didn't move. "You good?"

I nodded. "Yep."

He led me over to the Japan stand, where there was, in fact, a lavender tea and ramen booth. We each ordered both, but were told the wait would be about 20 minutes, it was a long line and the ramen was being cooked fresh.

"Let's go look at the kimonos," Colin suggested.

"Okay." We walked to the nearby clothing racks and started sifting through the bright colored kimonos. I pulled one out that was bright pink with white cherry blossoms on it. I hadn't worn anything that bright in years. "This is pretty."

Suddenly, Colin was right behind me looking over my shoulder. He was so close I was melting. "It's really nice."

"Want to try it on?" We looked over and a stall worker had wandered over. "We have a changing room."

"Try it on," Colin said. "We have time."

I felt embarrassed. "I don't know."

"Come on. We have to buy *something* with this money your mom gave us." I could see the excitement behind his eyes and it emboldened me.

I went back to the makeshift changing room between curtains in the back of the stall and wrapped the kimono around myself. I did my best to tie the sash in its traditional manner, but I was failing. I stepped out of the changing room and the saleswoman took over instantly, helping me tie the sash. I looked at myself in the mirror and it was weird seeing myself in such a bright color again, but I didn't hate it. I thought I probably would buy it, even if I never wore it. I started to undo the sash, but the saleswoman grabbed my hand.

"No, no. You have to show him." Started dragging me back towards Colin.

"Oh, no." I shook my head. "That's okay. I'm okay."

"Come on! He wants to see." She continued to pull me along, and given that she was a small, frail-looking old woman. I didn't want to just yank myself away, I'd break her. She pulled me through the stall and out towards the front, where Colin was standing looking through other articles of clothing. "Ta da!" she announced and it was so embarrassing.

Colin turned and looked at me and the look he gave me sent a shiver down my spine. His eyes shimmered like he was looking at a stack of pure gold and his lips parted just slightly, like he had the world to say, but didn't know how to say it. His emerald eyes drifted down my form slowly and back up again until they were locked in mine.

"Stunning." It was whispered, and came out almost like it was subconscious.

My skin was burning so much I thought it was going to melt off. "Y-yeah?"

Colin blinked. "Yeah. You have to get it."

I hadn't overcome my shock enough yet to do anything other than respond with an absent nod. I turned around and shuffled my way back to the changing room, my heart racing so hard I feared I was going to have a heart attack. I changed back into my regular clothes and walked back out to the front part of the stall. Colin was talking to a different salesperson and handing over some of his money. The woman who was helping me put the kimono in a bag and I started to pull out my wallet.

"Already paid for," the woman helping Colin said with a smile. "Your cute boyfriend did it."

Colin and I both started to stutter in response to the phrase, causing the woman who'd helped me to swat her on the arm. "Don't embarrass them! It's their first date."

I supposed the way we were behaving was very 'first date' like. I looked at Colin and he grinned at me and I couldn't help but smile back. Whether because we didn't feel like explaining our story to total strangers, or because somewhere inside us we liked to think their assumption was true, we decided not to correct them. Colin grabbed the bag with my kimono, we walked over and collected our tea and ramen, and found a spot to sit and eat.

The afternoon bled into the evening as we crawled the rest of the booths. We got sweets from Germany, including enough to bring back for my parents, took pictures at the fake Taj Mahal in India, and played with an adorable baby dingo that was promoting an animal rescue in Australia. Everything we did reminded us of some story from our childhood. He would start a story and then I would take it over and then he would take it over, and it would end with us laughing out loud about the tons of good times we'd had. The day ended better than I could have ever hoped for.

By the time we were pulling back into the driveway, the sun had already set. We walked inside, noticing that my parents were both passed out on the couch, and just decided to head upstairs. We got to our doors and came to a stop, facing each other, standing in the middle.

Colin smiled at me and handed the bag with the kimono over. "Thank you." His eyes were full of something spectacular. Something I'd seen before, but not for years. Something I'd once believed meant he loved me too. "This has been an amazing day."

"It really has. Thanks for coming with me."

I smiled up at Colin and I was reminded of the way we looked at each other that day he kissed me. I couldn't deny that I hoped this day would have the same outcome. Colin lifted his hand to my face and I took a breath in and held it. He brushed his thumb across my cheek, but just when I thought he may lean in, he rubbed his fingers and pulled his hand away.

"Still had a piece of glitter hanging out from

that one stand." It was a lie, but I didn't push it. "Well. Goodnight."

"Yeah. You too."

Colin turned around and went into his room and I finally let out my breath and fled to mine. I held my chest, trying to calm it's clamor. Even all this time later, Colin was still the only one who could make me feel so calm and so crazy all at once.

## 14

## COLIN

I smiled watching Tatiana flip through her phone, showing her mom the pictures we'd taken on Saturday. I was chewing away at the breakfast burritos her dad made us, and for the first time since I'd lost my parents, I felt at peace. I wasn't quite sure what Saturday meant for Tatiana and I, but there was something I saw very plainly that day.

Tatiana had feelings for me too.

I saw it in the way she looked at me, in the way she held her breath when we were standing outside our bedroom doors. It was the exact same look she'd given me that day at the mall. She was waiting for me to kiss her, and god knows I wanted to. After the day we'd had and the way she was staring at me like I could have asked her anything and gotten a positive response, I wanted to kiss her and I wanted to do more than that. I'd done a lot of growing up in five years, and whereas the Colin of five years ago was more than happy to kiss Tatiana alone, the current version of me wasn't sure I could control myself. She'd looked so fantastic in that kimono, and though I respected her greatly, there was a huge part of me that could only imagine peeling it off of her.

"Colin!"

I jumped to attention. "Huh?"

Tatiana tilted her head. "Jeez, where were you? I called your name like four times."

"Sorry. Just lost in thought I guess. What's up?"

Tatiana sat down next to me and picked up her breakfast burrito. "I was telling my mom about the tea. It was really good, wasn't it?"

"Oh, yeah!" I took the last bite of my food. "I mean, lavender tea was always Tati's favorite, but it was good."

Kya smiled at me. "I'm glad you two had such a good time."

It was already Monday, time to head back to school. It felt like the weekend had flown by having spent the day with Tatiana on Saturday, and then most of Sunday in my room doing homework and generally trying to turn down the fire raging inside me. The more I thought of Tatiana, the more I wanted her. I hadn't anticipated that little hiccup. Obviously rekindling an old flame from middle school would come with some new hat tricks. I'd lost my virginity the year prior to Harlie, and I knew that Tatiana was sleeping with Mr. Kepler. Neither of us was 'pure' so to speak, but we hadn't ever been together, and once I realized that, I couldn't drag my mind off of it.

"Tati, you talked for too long. Wrap it to go," Cristiano instructed.

Tatiana nodded and hopped off of the barstool and walked over to the other side of the island. I tried to keep my gaze safe, but as Tatiana stretched to try and get the tin foil down from on top of the fridge, her ass was right at eye length, and the base of her long-sleeved shirt separated dangerously from the top of her leggings, revealing just a glimpse of her silky stomach. I could feel all of my consciousness traveling south. I hadn't really helped myself out in the sexual department since Harlie and I broke up, and it was obvious that was going to have to change if I was going to continue being around this renewed Tatiana.

To my left, a loud clang jolted me. I looked up and Cristiano had his hand on his coffee mug, which was still rattling on the island countertop. His knuckles were white around the handle and he was leering down at me like he was going to bite my head off.

I'd been caught.

"Cris, everything okay?" Kya asked.

In a flash, the threatening stare was gone, and Cristiano's calm, friendly smile was back. "Yeah, just dropped my mug a little too hard."

I stared down at my plate. *Message received, Mr. Marquette.* I'd definitely need to be more careful. The Marquettes had been so good to me, and Tatiana and I were finally getting back to an okay place. The last thing I needed to do was risk it all because I was unable to keep my eyes in their sockets.

Tatiana and I were relatively chatty on the short car ride to school. It only took about three minutes by car to get there, but the entire time Tatiana and I exchanged playful jabs about our school work, Tatiana had gotten hers done in a couple of hours in the morning while I had to spend most of my Sunday getting mine done. It wasn't until Cristiano innocently made a comment about Tatiana still needing help in science. It brought the situation careening back at me like whiplash. Spending a nice Saturday with Tatiana had completely erased it from my brain; she was sleeping with a teacher. Maybe, now that we were doing pretty good again, I could talk to her about it. I didn't want to run in assuming she was blindly being taken advantage of, she certainly didn't seem forced when I saw her at the game, but any adult sleeping with a teenager was taking advantage of their naivety, that was a given.

When we pulled to a stop in front of the school, Cristiano smiled at us. "I'm glad you two are doing better. Have a good day at school."

"Thanks dad," Tatiana replied, and there was a certain lightness to her voice, like an iron weight had been lifted out.

We got out of the car, waved goodbye to Cristiano, and walked into school. I was trying to think of the best way to at least breach the subject of Tatiana's romantic life with her when she stopped moving. I glanced back and noticed she had a look of bewilderment on her face. I turned back around and saw that everyone in the hallways, who had seconds before been checking their lockers, chattering with friends, and bustling to class, were all frozen in place and staring at Tatiana. My stomach tightened.

*Uh oh.* I was anxiously searching the crowd for even one person not staring, but there were none.

All eyes were on Tatiana and I feared that I knew why.

"Why haven't you been answering my calls?!" One of the kids known for being a bit of a loser around school, Billy Benton, was rushing up to Tatiana, his face drenched in sweat and frightened. "I need to talk to you." Tatiana opened her mouth to reply, but Billy had already taken her by the wrist and was dragging her away.

Once Tatiana was out of sight, I started to panic. My forehead was already covered in sweat, as Billy's had been, and I was scanning the crowd for Harlie; I had to find her. It was a huge mistake telling her about Tatiana. I was impulsive. I should have just waited. The second she figured it out, I knew she was going to let the cat out of the bag, I just didn't realize the scale. She told everyone in school? *Everyone?*

There was a tap on my shoulder and I turned around to see our principal, Marcellus Devine, standing behind me. "Mr. Undinger. Can I speak to you in my office, please?"

*Shit.* "Sure." *Shit. Shit.*

I followed Mr. Devine, and even as I walked through the school office, all the teachers and administrators inside were staring at me. The *entire* school knew, staff included. This was bad. This was so bad. We walked into his personal office and he shut the door behind him. He motioned for me to sit in one of the stock school, gray, polyester armchairs sitting in front of his oak wood desk. He sat down in his chair and faced me and my heart was pounding harder and faster than it ever had before.

"What's up?" I asked, trying to remain even toned. "If this is about my parents. I'm actually doing well." Was I talking too much? Was it dumb to try and play innocent?

"That's not what this is about, though I'm glad to hear you're doing okay." He sighed. "No, this is about a different troubling matter. A rather disturbing rumor has made its way to me that your friend, Tatiana Marquette, is involved in, at the very least, a sexual relationship with one of our teachers here, Val Kepler. I've followed it as far back as I can and have learned from Harlie Jones that she heard this rumor from you."

There goes that hope of ever rekindling. Not only did she throw me under the bus by telling the school about Tatiana when she promised she wouldn't, she backed over me by telling the principal the rumor started with me. If she had told him, she probably told the rest of the school *that* part of the story as well.

"I don't know what you're talking about," I lied, praying I was convincing. "That's insane."

Mr. Devine raised his eyebrow, and I could tell he wasn't buying it. "Really?"

I shrugged. "Really."

"You know, Mr. Undinger. If there's any validity to these rumors, even if just a piece of the story, your friend could be in danger. If you know anything, you should say something. She could need help." He folded his hands on the desk in front of him, trying to do the 'concerned adult' bit. "I just want to be that help."

I knew that Tatiana needed help, but this wasn't how I wanted to do it. All I could picture was our amazing day out on Saturday and how much better we were doing, and it was all going up in smoke. If Tatiana found out I was the source of the rumor, I could kiss any hope of being *anything* to her--friends, lovers, or otherwise--goodbye.

I needed to make Mr. Devine believe me somehow. I didn't know if it was better to try and discuss what I'd seen, but belittle it by saying that I was mad at her and just made assumptions to hurt her, or continue to pretend as if I didn't know anything about the rumor at all.

"Look, Mr. D. I don't know what Harlie told you, but I didn't start any rumor about Tatiana seeing a teacher. I never would, because I know her really well, and I know she'd never do anything like that. The rumors were probably started by Harlie because she doesn't like Tatiana very much." An idea clicked into my head like a lightbulb turning on. "Harlie's my ex and I think she found out Tatiana and I went out on a date." I never wanted to be that guy that lied and said his interactions with a certain girl were more than they were, but I think Tatiana would agree this was an emergency.

Mr. Devine leaned in with renewed curiosity. "You're dating Miss Marquette?"

"Yeah. We went to that food festival this weekend." I pulled out my phone and flipped to the pictures we'd taken and handed it over. "See?"

Mr. Devine took my phone and started scrolling through the pictures. Eventually he handed it back to me, with a sigh of relief. "Well, that certainly sheds some light on things. I haven't spoken with Val Kepler yet, I know children can gossip and didn't want to involve him until I was certain. Just a jealous ex-girlfriend, eh?"

I felt like I was gonna throw up. "Yeah. Harlie's really vindictive, so she probably started the rumor and then told everyone I did to try and cause problems." As the words came out of me, I realized that they were probably true, even if I was spinning an untrue tale with those threads. "If I don't get to Tatiana before these rumors do, it's probably going to work."

Mr. Devine nodded. "Go. Go find her. I can't stop the rumors, but I'll let the rest of the staff know so we can try and dwarf them as much as we can."

I stood up from the chair desperate to get to Tatiana and warn her. "Thank you."

I started for the door when I was struck with another fear. I turned around and looked back at Mr. Devine. "Um. You're not going to call Tatiana's parents are you?"

Mr. Devine leaned back in his chair. "Do I need to?"

I shook my head. "No. Things are just really weird at her place right now, with me moving in and my parents' death and all that. I just don't want things to get worse because of some rumor a jealous ex of mine started."

Mr. Devine nodded. "I understand, Mr. Undinger. We'll keep this between us."

That time, it was me letting out a sigh of relief. "Thank you so much."

"Go find her," Mr. Devine said. "Hopefully it isn't too late." No kidding.

I rushed out of the office trying to figure out

where Billy might have pulled Tatiana off to, but I didn't need to search far. The second I opened the door, Tatiana walked up to me. Her eyes were puffy and red, and tears were still leaking from them.

"Tati," I murmured.

She looked at me as though I'd stuck a heated butcher knife straight through her. "How could you start such a terrible rumor about me?"

I took Tatiana's hand in mine and dragged her out through the front door. The teacher that normally monitored the door didn't stop us. He, too, had probably heard the rumors and figured we could use the space, or maybe he was too shy to intervene. In any event, I pulled her down the sidewalk and turned her to face me. She was still crying and it was breaking my heart.

"How could you say something so horrible about me?" she whimpered.

"I did not start this rumor," I put my hands on each of her shoulders, "but I know it's true."

Tatiana's eyes widened. "It's not."

"Yes it is. I saw you two at my game. I was

benched for the whole second half of the game and I saw you two go behind the bleachers. When you came out, he smacked you on your ass. You even got mad at him because he tried to kiss you out in the open. I saw the whole thing." Tatiana was looking at me with parted lips and glossy eyes like she was replaying it as I said it. "I knew that it was true, but I made the mistake of talking to Harlie about it--"

"You told Harlie?!" Her cheeks were darker than the rest of her face, but I didn't know if rage or embarrassment was the cause of the hue. "I--you--it..." She turned her back to me and started off towards her house.

I walked off after her, and when she realized I was following her, she took off running. I ran after her, and I may have been a quarterback on a varsity football team, but Tatiana was tiny, and she was fast. I just barely managed to keep up with her, and if it weren't for the struggle she experienced, she might have successfully locked me out when she bolted inside and attempted to slam the door in my face. I stuck my hand out and caught the door as it was closing and forced it back open. She abandoned that door and rushed up the stairs towards the bedrooms. I followed after her, taking the stairs two at a time, and fortunately caught her bedroom door as she attempted the same tactic as the front door.

I pushed my way into Tatiana's room and she turned around to face me, her expression full of rage and anguish. "Get out!"

"No! Just let me talk to you about this! I want to help you!"

"I don't need help. I'm fine!"

I dropped my jaw. "No you're not! You're sleeping with a teacher. He's got you brainwashed into thinking this is okay, when it isn't. It's toxic."

"You're one to talk!" Tatiana snapped.

"What's that supposed to mean?"

"You're toxic! I never know what you're thinking. One day you're one way, the next day you're another."

I felt like I was hearing all the things I should be yelling. "And you *don't* do that? One day you're barking at me about some petty comment you heard at school and then the next day you're asking me out! Pick a fucking lane!"

"You pick a lane!" Tatiana screamed back at me. "You're so hot and cold. It's just like that day you played with my emotions back in the 7th grade! You've always been that way."

My world stopped turning and everything in my brain toppled over. "Wait. What?"

"What?!"

"Me?" I couldn't find up or down all of a sudden. "*You* played with *my* emotions. I thought you wanted to be my girlfriend after I kissed you. The next thing I know, you're throwing your locket in the dirt and saying that being my girlfriend would be gross."

Tatiana took a step back, her expression matching how I felt. "Y-you… I only said that because you were all gung ho to go with that random girl to Sadie Hawkins and agreed to go on a date with her."

I felt like I was having an out of body experience. "What? When did I ever agree to go with anyone anywhere? The only girl I liked was you."

Tatiana was staring at me like she couldn't believe what I was saying. "I watched you." Her voice was no longer loud and forceful, but a confused murmur. "She asked you out and you said yes and when she asked you to Sadie Hawkins you said maybe."

The day started playing back in my head. I'd just found out that I made the football team and I was so elated I couldn't think straight. Between kissing Tatiana for the first time and finally being on the team I'd dreamed about for years, I was delirious. I could only think about getting to

Tatiana and celebrating with her; asking her to be my girlfriend and starting our new relationship. There were tons of people asking me to hang out and do stuff with them. I figured it just came with the territory since I'd made the team. My parents would have killed me for being rude to anyone. I had no recollection of any specific girl asking me out, but if one had, I would have agreed just to get them to stop talking to me so I could fast-track getting to Tatiana. 7th grade me didn't think about the consequences of stuff like that, only doing what made him happy. Tatiana made him happy.

"I don't remember that," I replied finally. "I mean, I remember lots of kids asking if I wanted to be friends all of a sudden and going out and stuff like that. I didn't want to get into any complicated conversations because it would have delayed me getting to you."

Silence fell between us. The same realization was giving us both uppercuts to the jaw. She misconstrued an interaction between me and one of the girls that was talking to me, so she said something she didn't mean? The past five years, being together, it had all been ruined because of a simple misunderstanding?

Tatiana turned her back to me. "Please leave."

I wouldn't--I couldn't. Learning what we just

had, how could I leave after that? Tatiana loved me too, she always had. "No."

"Colin!" she screamed and I could hear the tearful shake to her voice. "Leave!"

"No!" I grabbed her hand and whipped her around to face me. I pulled her close and looked down into those deep, intoxicating brown eyes, holding her in my arms fully for the first time. "If you can tell me to go one more time, I'll leave."

I could feel Tatiana's heart racing to match my own. Tears streamed down her face. "I hate you."

I shook my head. "No you don't." I pulled her face to mine and our lips met.

Nothing else mattered in that moment as I finally kissed Tatiana with all of our cards on the table.

## 16

# TATIANA

**M**y mind was a tornado, taking everything in its path off the ground, and refusing to set it back down. Colin's lips against mine were soft and sweet, a feeling I both recognized and didn't know. He'd grown. Even though I wouldn't consider our first kiss bad by any stretch, almost-adult Colin was a tsunami. He knew when to part his lips gently, when to lick his tongue out to slide along my bottom lip. He knew how to settle his hand just on the small of my back so that I could feel his heat all the way up my spine, and just how to tilt my face up ever so slightly, giving himself better access.

The emotions I'd locked away within me were clamoring at the bars, and the metal was bending.

It was as Colin had marched straight to the center of my brain and caused a sonic boom where he was standing. Everything got pushed further and further away with each additional second he was pressed against me, and even the few strands of logic that still hung on, that knew I should stop kissing Colin and tell him to leave, were overwhelmed by all the other ones that had waited *years* to kiss him again.

I tried to send a directive to my hands to push Colin away, but they locked behind his neck instead, attempting to eliminate what few remaining atoms stood between us. My legs journeyed backwards, taking us over to my bed where my legs defied their given orders as well and left the ground, taking Colin with, as I landed on my gray comforter. Colin melded his body to mine, his lips never parting from mine for a moment. Our speeding heartbeats were zooming along the same track. Colin's voice wisped into me in a breathless moan and the last shred of my resistance snapped. I wanted him so badly. Having him on top of me was unlike anything I'd experienced in my life. I thought of Val and the rumors flying around at school, but those thoughts were flies battering against a closed window. I was lost in Colin, too deep already, probably from the second he entered my room.

I felt like I couldn't breathe, but also like air wouldn't help me. Colin's cool hands snuck under the base of my shirt and rested directly against the skin of my stomach. My consciousness made a hard collision with the fact that it wasn't just about kissing anymore. 7th grade me wasn't around to help me anymore, I was in uncharted territory. Even as I thought I was making a mistake I'd never be able to recover from, I leaned into Colin's touch, bucked against him when his excited lower half found mine even through the four layers of fabric that separated us.

My everyday self had shut down completely and the backup drive I was working with only knew how to toss out breathless moans as Colin moved from my mouth to my neck and lower. The most sensitive parts of my body were screaming, demanding more. His tongue found places over my chest that had been visited before, but never with such passion. The pleasure wrapped itself around me in thick, heavy bands and I was bound to Colin by them. Why was I pulling his shirt up his torso and over his head? Why was I relenting as his hands traveled under me to my back to flick the clasps of my bra undone? Why were my fingers sewing into his hair to pull against him as though I was starving and he was the only food that would satiate?

"Tatiana."

This voice crawled over me like the slow, hot melting of wax down a candlestick. I continued to hear it long after his mouth was kissing its way down my stomach. I took a deep breath in and held it while Colin's hands undid the button of my jeans. Were we just now crossing the point of no return? No. When had we? Was it when he kissed me? Was it when he entered the house?

Or was it back when my mother first brought me to meet with Colin and his mom when we were babies? Destiny had charted our paths long before we were born. We stumbled along the path, face planted even, but was this truly where the road was meant to lead?

Colin rolled my pants down my legs, taking my underwear with them. I was so exposed I felt like I was laying on a bed of hot coals. He stood up to remove his own pants and we stared at each other in labored silence. Neither of us knew where we were anymore, only that we were there together, and that's what there was to latch onto. Colin positioned himself between my legs. His hardness poking at me below was nothing compared to the way his hand reached out and settled on my cheek.

He looked at me as if he thought he might awaken at any moment. I grabbed his hips and pulled, my body defying me yet again.

His hand rigidified against my face and he closed his eyes as he worked his way in. My mouth opened to allow sound to escape, but nothing came out. The walls of my bedroom faded away and the furniture disappeared. I got such severe tunnel vision that I wouldn't have even drawn myself into this scene if I were asked to recreate it. Colin was it. His chest rising and falling, his jaw clenching, his resistant movements. Was he just trying to make it last?

Every piece of me started to hum their own notes of enjoyment as Colin worked. It was slow, but intense, and the more he rocked, the louder the hums got, the closer they got, until they were all laced together in a single harmony; loud and powerful. My legs shook despite my begging them not to, and then the sound that had barricaded itself back before, warbled out of me in the shape of Colin's name. He held on tight, traversing through my shaking pleasure, and the look on his face suggesting it was his body battling against his wishes now.

"Shit," he whispered.

My hands walked up Colin's arms and over his

wide shoulders, to nestle themselves into the grooves on his back. I pulled and he blanketed himself over me. Our mouths met again, and with Colin finally dialing up the pace, I could hear the hums again. This time, they started out in harmony, but the harmonies themselves multiplied. They got louder and more prevalent, forming a song headed quickly for the bridge. I let out a scream as the song amplified to the point that I lost all feeling and could only hear a loose, white ringing in my ears. I was fighting to catch my breath, with Colin struggling to take short breaths as well. My mind couldn't find purchase. I'd just had sex with Colin and every attempt I made to make sense of that fact was resulting in a critical error.

The thoughts of Val finally forced his way through the closed window and when I saw them, I came colliding back to earth in a sobering, painful slam. I'd just cheated on him. I'd been wrong about Colin for five years and slept with him without giving it a second thought. My life's intentions, which had been neatly arranged before, were now a mess all over the floor. I felt like I was going to be sick.

Colin looked down at me and I didn't know what to tell him. When I opened my mouth, the only words that came out, "I just made a huge mistake," could have referred to anything, but the words slapped Colin across the face so hard I expected it to bruise.

His movements were hasty and clumsy as he left my body, gathered his clothes, and left. The subsequent cold that strangled me couldn't have been warmed if I doused myself in flames. I didn't move and allowed the waterfalls of tears careening down my cheeks to move unfettered. I *had* made a huge mistake, I'd made several, and I had no clue how to fix any one of them.

## 17

## TATIANA

I had barely moved in several days; I was numb. I'd spent two days pretending I was sick and trying to figure out how to turn my brain off. Any time it was on, if I was aware of my consciousness even a little bit, the feeling of Colin's body on mine came smashing back into me. I was already of the new, permanent yearning my body had, as if I had been born with Colin attached to me, and now that he was gone, it was like part of me was missing too. I hadn't even seen his perfectly cut abs, or the flawless framing of his hair around his lush covered face. My lower region tingled hungrily every time it crossed my mind, which was constant. I wasn't walking on my own two feet anymore. When Colin left, I needed crutches, and it infuriated me. Since when was he *that* big of an influence over me? How did he manage to leave so much of his heat behind? How could I get back to the Tatiana of a few days ago? Did that girl even exist anymore?

"Tati." A knock on my door followed my father's gruff voice. "I made the soup."

Good. I was starving. There aren't many illnesses one can fake that can't be verified. I had to go for stomach flu with a loss of appetite, so I'd avoided eating to convince my parents of the lie. It wasn't like it mattered. No amount of food that traveled down my throat could calm the braying hunger situated deep inside of me. The food I required now was entirely different from what I needed before. Each day I gave my body something different, it forced me to endure more dreams of Colin's eyes bearing down on me while taking me whole, rousing me from my sleep with a frustrating moisture between my legs and a devilish desire to sneak across the hall.

"Thanks." I supposed I could move for soup. Even if I now wanted something different from what I'd find in a bowl downstairs, my dad's soup had a magical ability to soothe the soul, and if nothing else I wouldn't pass out from depriving my body of nutrition. "Coming."

I forced myself out of bed with my feet finding

the floor in pitiful clomps. I was sloth-like in my trudges out of my bedroom, down the stairs, and into the kitchen where my father was putting a healthy serving of his homemade chicken noodle soup into a bowl. He had taken the day off to stay home with me. A couple days of being sick was one thing, but by day three they were worried enough to think I needed an overseer. They believed that I'd been brought home from school on Monday by Colin because he thought I was sick and didn't want to leave me alone. This was no doubt the lie he told them when they inquired about our communal absence. In any other situation, I could have had Val fudge the numbers for me, but I wasn't talking to him either for the moment, purely from embarrassment. I wasn't going to call him to ask for a favor when I'd been avoiding him, especially when the reason I was avoiding him was because I'd stepped out on him and didn't want him to find out. That'd see me cross from cold to straight up heartless.

"How ya feeling?" My dad asked, breaking through my thoughts.

I lapped at my soup, the spoon barely serving its purpose to be a go-between the food and my mouth. "A little better I guess." In retrospect I had to start "getting better" otherwise they'd drag me into a doctor when I wasn't even sick--well not the kind of sick a health practitioner could help with.

"That's good." He walked over to the fridge and used its auto-ice and water dispenser to get me a glass of water. "It might be a good idea to get some fresh air at some point."

I literally never liked fresh air. "Maybe?"

"Colin has a game tonight." Just hearing his name was like a tennis racket to the face. "You should come along. It could do some good. You and Colin are friends again, so it's okay, right?"

"Uh, erm, um…" I tried to find any viable lie that would take hold, but I was struggling. "I don't know."

My dad looked into me in a way that let me know he was aware of more than he was letting on. "You and Colin were doing so well, but now you haven't spoken in days."

"I've been sick." I swallowed hard. Parents. Where did they get their mystical abilities to know everything. Was there a parent store they could purchase the upgrade from, or did it hit them after their kid was born, like puberty? "I didn't want to make him sick too."

My dad crossed his arms. "Did something happen at school?"

I did my best to maintain my 'sick' demeanor. "No, why?"

"You've been sick before and have gone to school anyway." He shrugged and turned his back to me to wash a few dishes that I knew he didn't actually care about the current cleanliness of. "It's no matter. I'll ask Colin about it."

*No, no, no.* Colin was powerless in front of my parents, and that was even before he felt like they owed them this huge debt. If my dad talked to him and he pushed enough, there was a very high possibility Colin would come clean, about us sleeping together, or possibly even about Val, and I couldn't risk any of that.

"Dad, really, I'm just not feeling good." I swallowed my disdain for attending that damn football game. "It's a good idea. I'll go to the game."

My dad tossed me a victorious smirk. "Good!"

*Ass.* The little game we'd just played had gone exactly as he intended it to.

The rest of the day passed in the blink of an eye. I wanted it to go slower so I could prepare myself mentally to see Colin again, but every time I turned around, another hour had ticked by. Before long, I was arguing with myself about how nicely to dress while simultaneously trying to decide how much of my own comfort I was willing to sacrifice.

In the end, I landed on a pair of black leggings with dark purple and blue flowers up the sides of the legs. I wore a pair of dark green, laced, combat boots and a dark green windbreaker that would both keep me warm, and hugged my frame in a subtle, yet appealing way. I tried not to think about the fact that I was doing myself up for Colin when I still hadn't sorted out what our relationship even was yet. *It's just nice to look nice.* At least that's what I told myself.

We were at the school an hour later, walking through the cold autumn air. We found my parents' favorite spot on the bleachers, front row, center, where it was easy for Colin to see us. We sat and, at first, I thought I was going to be okay, but then the football team came out. Fuck my brain for making Colin run across the field in slow motion like David Hasselhoff in Baywatch. His hair was fluttering in the wind and I actually caught myself looking around to see if anyone else was seeing it the same way I was, or if I was really and truly that drunk on him. Most everyone was still on their phones or chatting away with the people around them.

Just me then? Perfect.

Colin led his team over to the bench and the game began shortly thereafter. Colin was the quarterback, which meant he was the most important player on the team. As the first quarter kicked into action, there were plenty of moments where all of the attention was on him. Blazing the ball down the field in a powerful throw, filling in as a tackle and keeping some defensive lineman at bay. Even under his helmet and pads, every time he moved it was like it rocketed across the earth to shake me and me alone. His hands on the ball reminded me of the way he curled his fingers around my legs to hold me in place. Every time he crouched to prepare for the snap, my mind fled back to him crouched in front of me, naked and breathing hard.

Wasn't it cold just a few minutes ago? Why was I burning up?

The crowd started to roar when, near the end of the first quarter, Colin found a crack in the defense and decided to run the ball downfield himself as opposed to throwing it or handing it off. He snaked his way between the linemen until he was well downfield and the density of the opposing team's players got thinner and thinner. Colin blasted through until he was out in front of the team and charging towards his end zone with not a defensive player in sight. He crossed into the endzone and the bleachers erupted.

"And that was Colin Undinger with an impressive 52-yard run to bring the Tigers into the lead!"

The announcer screamed into the sound system. "And that's halftime. Let's hear it for number 22!"

The spectators started to chant Colin's name and he responded by pulling off his helmet, letting his brown hair spill out and down to his shoulders, and then he smiled and waved. It coiled around my neck and strangled me. Why was being on the same *football field* so hard? I was going to have to sort things out with him sooner than I was planning on. I needed my freedom to breathe and think about something other than him back.

"I need a drink." I stood up, not even waiting for my parents to respond, and walked down off the bleachers. Orchard Mesa wasn't the fanciest school around, but it had a concession stand with a reasonable selection of beverages. Unfortunately, none of them were alcoholic.

I got into the line behind the stand and fished some cash out of my pocket. I was reviewing the menu, trying to decide exactly what I thought would help most with my Colin-induced thirst, when a hand clamped around my arm. I looked over and there was a man attached to the arm, in a black hoodie with the hood pulled so far over, it was difficult to see who it was; but I knew who it was.

I relented as he pulled me out of the line and out of the sight and earshot of the other people at the game. He reached up and pushed the hood back a little, but not all the way, just enough for me to see his steel gray eyes.

"Val," I murmured. His hand was still clenched around my arm. "You shouldn't be here."

"Why haven't you been responding to my calls or texts?" His voice was a tone I was unused to. Rough as opposed to its normal silk. "How did people find out about us?"

His eyes had a crazed, far-out look that was frightening. "I guess a student saw us at the last game. I'm just trying not to get us in more trouble. I have to go, we can't be seen together." I turned to walk away, but Val's grip on my arm tightened and pulled me back to him. "That hurts. Let me go."

"Don't make a scene," Val growled at me. He wasn't the man I knew. "I know you're lying to me."

My heart skipped a beat. "What?" Had he somehow found out about Colin and I sleeping together? Did Colin tell someone? He wouldn't talk to Harlie again after how she fucked it up the first time, right?

"You're dating Colin Undinger." He yanked me closer to him. "The principal told me that Colin was able to confirm it, that's how he explained that we weren't sleeping together."

I tried to claw Val's hand off of me. "I don't know anything about that. Let me go."

Val leaned down until his face was centimeters from mine. His skin was paler than I'd ever seen it, and he radiated a forcefulness that made me feel like a gazelle cornered by a lion. "You had better think twice about stepping out on me. You're mine." His words weren't endearing or protective at all, they were possessive; obsessive.

My throat was tight and I felt like I was about to cry. I was the most afraid I'd ever been in my entire life. "I-I didn't. I love you. I wouldn't cheat on you." I could already feel tears gathering in the corners of my eyes.

Val's look of psychotic rage dissipated, and the more serene expression I was used to found him. It was forced out, though, like the Hulk trying to put his human shirt over his mutant body. "Good." He released my arm, though I could still feel the pain of the tight grip stinging against my skin. He rubbed a hand across my cheek. "Get some rest tonight. You've missed a lot of tutoring this week, and you owe me for all of the trouble you've caused."

## 18

## COLIN

C hecking my voicemails had been a mistake. Ordinarily, we weren't allowed to have our cell phones out in the locker room during games, even if it was halftime, but Coach Nash gave me a pass due to my special circumstances. Recently deceased parents, staying with a family that wasn't my own, the sudden influx of responsibilities I had to take on; there was more than one reason for me not to be able to ignore my phone for multiple hours in a row. Today happened to be one of those days where something did come in while I was playing the first half of the game, but I wish I hadn't checked. My parent's lawyer called to let me know that we needed to figure out what was going on with all the stuff my parents had left me in their wills and my aunt called because she's going to be back in Orchard Mesa and wanted to discuss my plans for my parents' restaurant. I was being pulled in all these directions a teenager was never meant to be pulled in. Throw all of these things in with how things had gone down with Tatiana earlier in the week and you've got yourself a regular distraction cocktail.

I was trying to keep my emotions in check, not wanting to get benched again, but as I was slipping my phone back into my bag and getting ready to go back out, Coach Nash approached me.

"Undinger, how've you been feeling?"

It was amusing that, even when he was coaching a football game, he could never really turn that school counselor part of him off. "I'm doing okay."

"You're playing better, but I can see you're still out of sorts." I must have shown my displeasure with the statement, because Coach Nash put his hand on my shoulder. "Relax, kid. After that touchdown, even if I wanted to pull you, I'd get a trash shower from the crowd. No, I just want to make sure everything is okay. I know that you're probably feeling like you don't have anyone to talk to and I want you to know, I'm here to help. I'm your counselor and your coach, but I'm also your friend. If you want someone to talk to, I promise anything you say stays with me."

I thought about the way things were piling up and his offer sounded good as gold. "That'd actually be really helpful, Coach."

Coach Nash nodded. "Good. After the game we'll chat with the Marquettes and then go grab a bite, sound good?"

I nodded. The idea of being able to actually talk to someone about all of the bullshit I was experiencing rejuvenated me a bit.

I was glad I wasn't being benched again, and it showed in my gameplay. I didn't get anything even close to my touchdown play from the first half, but by the fourth quarter, the opposing team had tied up the game. The final quarter of the game was a tit-for-tat game of advancing the ball a handful of yards and then turning it over. We'd each ramped up our defenses in preparation for pulling a victory out in the fourth quarter, and we sent the game into overtime. We just needed one good play, so I called an audible against Coach Nash's wishes, and tried for a hail mary. It worked, though by the skin of our teeth, and got us the points we needed to secure the victory. Everyone went wild, and when I looked over at the bleachers where the Marquettes were sitting, they were all on their feet cheering, even Tatiana. For a second, I felt like our eyes met, but then I started thinking about the impossibility with my helmet and decided it was just wishful thinking.

After I finally managed to work my way through the sea of people congratulating me on my gameplay, Coach Nash and I approached the Marquettes outside the field. Tatiana was sitting in the car with her headphones in. She glanced up at me when I approached the car, but quickly averted her gaze. I didn't know where to go from where we'd left things. I'd gathered from our blow up that Tatiana said things she didn't mean when she was hurt, but did she really think that sleeping with me was a mistake? All up until she said that, I was about to count that as the best day of my life.

Coach Nash explained to the Marquettes that he was going to be taking me out for a bite to catch up. The Marquettes were very open to the idea, but made sure that's what I wanted and I assured them that I did, and then we parted ways with Coach Nash promising not to have me home too late. We drove to a greasy burger joint near school that most of the students and staff loved to frequent. We placed orders for burgers and fries, the typical bro-talk meal, and then found a booth and sat down.

"Alright. Are you going to make me ask you

weird counselor questions first?" Coach Nash asked.

I shook my head. "I don't have the energy for that. Shit's rough right now, Coach."

"Well, start at the beginning." He took a fry and popped it in his mouth.

"Like, with my parents dying?"

He shook his head dramatically. "No! I know that part!" I chuckled at how uncomfortable the question made him and he smiled. "Oh, there's a smile. I'll take it. Alright, rephrase. Start just *after* the beginning."

"Well, the Marquette's daughter, Tatiana. I'm in love with her. Like dumb in love." It felt oddly satisfying saying it out loud. "My parents and hers were really close, so we've been friends since we were babies. Somewhere along the way, I just went crazy for her. In middle school there was this thing that happened and I thought she hated me, but I just found out on Monday that she thought I hated her. It was just a misunderstanding."

"Does she feel the same way about you?" Coach Nash asked.

I nodded. "I think so. I mean... I don't know. She's hard to read. We, uh... We slept together."

"I heard from the principal you guys were dating."

The lie I'd told the principal in the wake of being asked about Mr. Kepler and Tatiana came back to me. "Oh, right... Uh, that's not true."

"It's not?" he asked and then his eyes widened. "Wait... Does that mean the rumor is true?" He stopped eating entirely. "Is Val having sex with her?"

I looked at him, hoping I could trust him more than Harlie. "Yeah."

Coach Nash scrunched up his nose. "I always knew there was something off about that guy. I told them way back when they first hired him that he was too friendly with the female students."

My jaw dropped. "Wait, really? He's known for this?"

"Well, you know. No one ever wants to think that's happening. Especially not in a small town like ours, so they look for any excuse to pretend that it's not." He scoffed with disgust. "God, I wanna go find him and fucking throttle him. She's just a kid!"

Fear rocked me. "No! You can't tell anyone I told you! There's already the rumor at school and her parents don't know and I--"

"Whoa, whoa, whoa, Undinger. Breathe!" I took a breath, not realizing that I was so emotional about it. "I told you, didn't I? Everything we say here stays between us. Although, take a bit of advice from someone who's been through some shit. Tatiana's in trouble if she's mixed up with him. Anyone who is crazy enough to sleep with one of his teenage students probably doesn't have a 'crazy cap' if you know what I mean?"

That hadn't even occurred to me. I was so caught up in the fact that they were seeing each other at all that I didn't even consider what else could be wrong with the man. If Tatiana was in danger and I wasn't telling anyone who could actually help her, I would be personally responsible if something happened to her.

"I don't know what to do," I admitted. "First my parents, then everyone started tossing all of these responsibilities at me and asking me to make these big decisions, then all of this stuff with Tatiana. My parents just died a couple of weeks ago, but it feels like it's been months. I haven't even had a chance to mourn them. I feel like if I blink, something's gonna go wrong."

Coach Nash nodded. "That's normal. I mean it's not, no one should have to go through that, but given what's going on, your feelings are valid and expected. First of all, take some time to mourn your folks. However you gotta do it. Lock yourself in the shower and cry it out. Write them a letter. Visit their graves. It'll be painful, but I promise you'll feel better. All the responsibilities and decisions, just take 'em one at a time, and tell everyone so. You're a kid. You can't be expected to do all of that. Don't be afraid to tell people to back off, you can only navigate one thing at a time."

I took a deep breath. It made sense. I was trying to balance it all. I just needed to take it one step at a time. "Yeah."

"As for Tatiana, you two probably need to talk, but before that, you gotta figure out what to do about Val. I promised I won't say anything, but you do realize the position that puts me in as her counselor, and in general as a human being, right?" I nodded. I was aware.

"I'm going to tell her parents. Start there at least." I was confident as I said the words; I knew it was the right thing to do. "I'm going to tell her first though." I didn't want her getting any more surprises with my face on the wrapping paper. "She's gonna hate me."

Coach Nash put his hand on my shoulder. "Sometimes the ones we love can't see that we're doing what's best for them."

We finished dinner with Coach Nash giving me some more helpful advice and doing everything in his power to cheer me up a bit. It was the first time I'd really put the pain I was going through with my parents and Tatiana out of my mind and focused on being myself for a little bit. It was nice. I'd have to make sure I didn't stray too much further from myself trying to make heads or tails of the crazy world I'd found myself in. I needed to ground myself in who I was and what I stood for, and the rest should just fall into place.

At least I was hoping so.

Coach Nash dropped me off and I quietly snuck in through the front door, knowing the Marquette's penchant for falling asleep on the couch in their living room, and made my way up to Tatiana's room. I knocked a couple of times, but when I didn't get an answer, I just entered. When I walked in, she was sitting on her bed with her eyes closed and her headphones in. I didn't want to scare her, so I walked over and sat as gently as I could on the edge of her bed. She did jump a little and look over at me, immediately pulling her head-phones out.

"Hi." The expression on her face was weary and I might have been imagining it, but it almost looked as if she'd been crying. "Great game tonight."

"Thanks." I wanted to reach out and touch her so badly I was shaking, but I resisted the urge. "I need to tell you something. It's about Val."

The instant his name left my mouth, Tatiana's face twisted in anguish. The plans I'd made to bring the matter to her parents flew out the window the second she threw herself into my arms and immediately started to sob.

## 19

### TATIANA

I t had been a while since either Colin or I had said anything. I didn't expect to react the way I did, but the second I saw him I felt comforted. He was the one who always took care of me when we were younger. Sure, my parents were my parents and took care of me the way parents were meant to, but Colin was different. He made me feel safe. Just being there with him, laying in his arms as he gently threaded his fingers in and out of my hair, stopping a few times to massage my head, before repeating the cycle, made me feel like Val couldn't get to me. Colin had always made me feel that way; fearless, not because he made me feel bulletproof, but because I knew if anything happened to me, he'd be there to protect me.

He wasn't pressuring me to explain my sudden outburst, which I appreciated, because I wasn't sure what I was going to say. I didn't know if I should tell him the truth or if I should just brush it off as wanting to break up with Val and not knowing how. The idea of lying to Colin coated me like grime. I didn't want to be untruthful with him anymore. Not being honest with each other had already led to so many problems for us. For once, I just wanted to be open with him, and hopefully not by screaming at each other.

I shifted, trying to move so that I could look up at him. He was laying behind me, cradling me, but I needed those green eyes to look into mine and tell me everything would be okay. I rolled to one side, but my face skated a little too close to Colin's in the process. What was meant to be a simple reposition so that I could talk to him fully, ended with his lips on mine. He continued to slowly caress as we kissed, somehow telling me anyway that everything would be okay. He was warm, not in the way that the weather was warm, but in the way that Christmas decorations were warm, or hearing from an old friend after a long time. He was the opening my puzzle piece was designed to fit in, and when we were close, there was no denying it.

Sure, I wanted to talk to Colin, but it could

wait. Not the most intimate sex Val and I had ever had could make me feel the way Colin did with just the simplest of touches. Just as my hands had before, they linked behind Colin's neck and pulled him towards me, but this time, they did so with my permission. I wanted the familiar feeling of his body against mine, to only go to that place Colin had managed to take me. I could feel his resistance, even so much that he pulled up from me, but I put my hand on his face and looked deep into his green pools, assuring him that this time would not end as the other had. I wanted to be with him this time. I didn't want to trip and fall into it; this was deliberate.

He grinned at me and ducked his head back down to mine, this time leading with his tongue to push it between my lips to play with mine. I moaned against his lips. We were just kissing, that was it, but it was otherworldly. It was taking me outside myself, on a vacation far from the fear of the world I was in. I could have clung to it forever were it not for the interruption of a knock on my door.

"Tatiana?" Colin jumped up away from me, and for the first time in my entire life, I imagined hitting my mother with my dad's shitty Corolla.

"Yeah?" I barked back, and the severity made

Colin laugh. I smiled and softened a bit. I let my frustration with parting ways show, which gave him at least some confidence.

"Is Colin in there?" she asked, and Colin slid down off my bed and sat on the floor in front of it.

"Yep!" Colin replied.

The door opened, showing my mom's confidence that nothing untoward was happening inside, and she smiled. "Hi, sorry. I didn't realize you'd gotten home."

Colin rubbed his head, something of a nervous tick he had. "Yeah, I wasn't sure if you guys were sleeping or something, so I kind of snuck in."

"Oh no worries. I just wanted to tell you that I spoke with your parents lawyer. She--"

"Yeah," Colin cut her off, "I got her voicemail. She was talking about all of this stuff that I wasn't really ready to deal with. It overwhelmed me."

My mom got that protective, 'mama bear' smile she sometimes displayed when dealing with people who'd upset me. "Yes. I spoke with her. I told her that you are not yet 18, and we're your legal guardians for the time being, so any future requests need to come through us. I wasn't happy to hear she'd disturbed you during your game with that."

I grinned. My mom was pretty great. "Nice mom."

Colin was smiling too. "Thanks, Kya. I promise, I'll get it all figured out."

"*We'll* get it all figured out," my mom replied. "We'll work on it bit by bit over the next few weeks so that, when you turn 18, you'll be ready. Don't you worry." Colin glanced up at me, and even with my mom standing there, I reached a hand out and placed it on his head, scratching lightly. He leaned back into my touch and my mom smiled widely. "I suppose now's as good a time as any to ask, what would you like to do for your birthday?"

Colin's face screwed like he was confused. "Oh." I pet a little harder. It must have been washing over him that it was his first birthday without his parents. "I guess I hadn't thought about it."

"Well, we can do whatever you'd like. Family vacation, big party, anything." Colin didn't respond and my mom sensed she'd pushed too hard. "You don't have to answer now. Just think about it. Whatever you'd like to do, big or small, I'll make it happen."

Colin smiled again. "Thank you."

She looked at us with a blissful expression and then I watched as her gaze slowly drifted upwards. A silent 'we did it' to her late friend. "Well, I'll leave you two then. Don't stay up too late, it's still a school night."

"Thanks mom." I looked right at my mom and her grin grew. She walked out without another word.

Colin closed his eyes and I continued to pet his head. "Your parents are being too good to me."

"They just care about you a lot. Don't be afraid to ask for help when you need it."

Colin scoffed. "You should take your own advice."

"What?"

Colin turned around so he was on his knees leaning against the bed. "Something happened, I can see it."

Val's terrifying expression bled into my mind. "Val... He's not who I thought he was."

"What happened?"

I recounted the story to Colin, watching as he got angrier and angrier with each detail. Emotions swelled up in me again as fear tried to seep it's way back in. I looked at Colin and allowed his presence to soothe me.

"I could fucking kill that guy." He looked up at me. "I swear to god, if he hurts you…"

"Relax." I put my hand on his face. "You have plenty to worry about. I've got it handled."

Colin wasn't convinced. I laced my fingers into his hair again, and he was like a dog getting scratches behind the ear. He looked at me and it was plain to see he was conflicted about something. The amorous moment that had taken us before was gone, but the romance was as real as ever. Whatever was going on in his mind involved me. I wanted to ask, but left it be. Whatever it was, I got the feeling I wasn't quite ready to address it yet.

We stayed that way until Colin let out a yawn, and then I caught it and released one of my own. In the silence between us it was apparent, we wanted to stay together. He and I both knew why we couldn't for the time being, but it didn't quell the desire.

Colin kissed the top of my hand. "Goodnight, Tati."

I smiled. "Goodnight."

Colin stood up and walked towards the door, but when he got to it, he stopped. He turned and looked at me and his lips parted ever so slightly, but then they closed again. He gave me a final, calm grin before turning again and leaving.

"Yeah," I whispered after he was gone. "Me too."

## 20

## TATIANA

### Two Weeks Later...

I had no idea if my plan to wean myself off of Val, or rather him off of me, was a good one, but it was the best hope I had for the time being. He was already so erratic, that I didn't want to just quit him suddenly. If that triggered him, there was no telling what he would do. I figured it was in my best interest to slowly start seeing him less and less, talking to him more infrequently, and then when it's finally time to end it, he saw it coming. My thought process was that, if I cooled us off first, then the final dousing wouldn't hurt so much; maybe he wouldn't freak out the way he did at Colin's game. I'd planned to wait about two weeks and hopefully do it before Colin's birthday, which was the upcoming Saturday. Colin and I were in such a good place. We'd talked things out and, even though we hadn't said as much, we wanted to be together. Val was a huge roadblock and I was ready to get rid of it. The thought that I could tell Colin on his birthday that I was ready to be with him, excited me. All I had to do was break up with Val. I was down to seeing him only once a week, and today was the day. I had to do it now, or it wouldn't happen in time.

Colin.

He confessed to me that he wanted to tell my parents about my relationship with Val, but when it became apparent that I wanted to end things, he agreed to keep it quiet on the promise that I would deal with it, and I made immediate plans to do so. Val was the only thing that stood between Colin and I, so he had to go, plain and simple. The last two weeks were like a dream, or at the very least a setup for one. Colin and I hadn't confessed our feelings to one another in the obvious sense, but it was there. In our eyes locking when we walked out of our bedrooms in the morning, to the way Colin asked if we could start walking to school in the mornings to spend some time alone. From the way I gave up my typical barstool at the kitchen island during breakfast to sit at the one directly next to him, to the way we seemed to get lost in each other whenever we crossed paths in school. The rumor that Val and I were seeing each other had been replaced in full with the one that Colin and I were, and I was much less willing to try and shut that one down. It was my hope that one day soon it wouldn't be a rumor anymore. I could tell that Colin wished that too.

The only problem that could be identified with Colin and I, if there was one, was that we struggled to keep our hands off of one another when the opportunities presented themselves. Maybe we were just trying to make up for lost time, but what were meant to be quick pecks often resulted in us vertical on some surface or another. We could be quick in getting an article or two of clothing off before one of my parents appeared to ruin the party. Somewhere along the way, they'd both gathered that there was something more between us, and though they didn't take much issue with us being alone together in his room or mine, they would always find some reason to come talk to us once an hour or so. Things never got past making out despite how much we wanted them to. It was probably a good thing, I hadn't broken up with Val yet, so I was technically cheating on them both, but Colin was aware he was the only one I really wanted. If any of those chances to be with him had successfully happened, I would have done so with not a shred of remorse.

I stood outside of Val's door wishing that it was going to be Colin waiting for me on the other side. I thought of Colin and the promise of being with him without worries and it pumped confidence in me to do what I had to do. I knocked on the door and entered without waiting for a response. Val was anticipating my arrival, he always was.

When I entered, he looked up at me, but didn't smile. "Lock the door."

I was hoping he wouldn't go straight for ground zero, but I might have expected as much. "We shouldn't," I responded. "I know the rumors have died down some, but--"

Val's chair screeching across the floor was loud and unexpected. He stormed across the room, reached around me and locked the door. With a hand on my waist, he forced me up against the door and leaned so close I could feel the warmth of his breath on my face. "You don't think we should, or you don't want to?"

I didn't want to. Val's fingers dug into my flesh and it hurt. "You're hurting me."

"Answer the question. You've been coming to

see me less, you don't reply to my texts." An animalistic grunt boiled out. "Tell me the truth, you're cheating on me with Colin Undinger aren't you?"

All of my certainty that I could turn Val away abandoned me in an instant. I just wanted to end things with him, but I had no way of guaranteeing he wouldn't bite my head clean off my shoulders if I did it right here, right now. I was scared, and couldn't bring myself to make him any angrier by admitting that I was cheating on him, or even just ending things amicably.

"I-I'm not," I whimpered.

Val's hand tightened. "Really?" Disbelief rode out on huffs through his nose; a dragon about to breathe fire.

"R-Really." I did the best I could to shift under Val's restraint. There were going to be bruises if I didn't move soon.

"Prove it." Val's hand slipped up from its spot on my waist and under my shirt. I tried to remember what it felt like to have his hands on my skin before. Did it always feel so *diseased?*

I put my hands on his chest and pushed. "We shouldn't do it here anymore. Not with what people already think."

Val pulled away a little, to my surprise, looking

down at me with some of his anger being replaced with desperation. "This is the only place I see you anymore. You've spent the last few weekends at home."

My sneaking out to see Val had come to a screeching halt the day Colin's parents died. At first it was the confusion at home, then it was the fear of being caught, fast-forward to Colin and I spending the day at the food festival a couple of weeks ago, and I was looking for any opportunity to spend my days with him. Val had picked up on it, which wasn't shocking, but didn't help my case at all, well it did, but it didn't make him less angry.

"It's my parents." I banked on being able to hide a lie despite my general lack of control over the situation. "Ever since Colin first moved in, they want me home all the time."

Oddly enough, Val seemed to accept the excuse. "But if we can't be together here, and we can't be together at my house…" Val's hand dug into the bare skin of my stomach now. "When are we going to be together?"

I'd suddenly found myself at a crossroads. Val had presented the perfect door for me to walk through. *I don't think we can be together.* It was an ideal breakup scenario, apart from the fact that I was alone with him in a dark, locked room that no one else was expected to be in again until the next day. More likely than not, no one even saw me come in. If Val snapped and did something crazy, no one would know at least until my parents started to suspect I should be home, but Colin had an away game that night and they were planning on making the journey. Val could kill and bury me before anyone realized it.

I was trying to convince myself that I was being overly dramatic. Val was maybe a little obsessive, but he wasn't a psycho. He wouldn't hurt me, certainly not kill me.

Still, maybe ending things was best done in a public place.

"You're right." I put a shaky hand to his face. "We shouldn't do it here, but let's meet up on Sunday."

"I don't want to wait that long," Val replied. "Saturday."

My heart pounded. "I can't on Saturday. My parents are holding a birthday party for… Colin." My stomach screamed out in pain as Val's fingers hooked even deeper into me, threatening to puncture the skin. I winced, but kept my hand on Val's face. "Hey, calm down. I wish I could come on Saturday, but if I'm not there, they'll ask questions.

Please just be patient and I'll spend all day on Sunday with you."

Val's hold loosened and my mind went a little fuzzy as I tried to shake away the ache. He took a deep breath and as he breathed out, all of his frightening behavior went with it. He opened his eyes and he was back to looking like the Val I knew, with nothing but caring kindness inside of him. He kissed my cheek and then let his forehead drop to my shoulder.

"I'm sorry for acting this way. I just love you so much. I can't imagine losing you." His hand gently smoothed over the part of my flesh he'd been torturing moments before. "Please spend Sunday with me."

I hugged him, just looking for any excuse to get out of the room. "It's okay. I love you too. I should probably go, but Sunday, okay?"

Val leaned back, a small smile on his face. "Okay."

I allowed him to kiss me briefly and then I gathered my things and left. I felt compelled to run as fast as I could, but I held back and walked at a normal pace down the empty after school hallways and eventually out through the front door. My heart was still pounding and I wished that Colin was there to walk with me home. It wasn't just that I'd grown used to having him by my side on walks to and from school, I always wanted to see him most after I had to deal with Val. I assumed that things with Val had to feel good at some point, otherwise I wouldn't have done it. Was I just that blinded by my heartache with Colin even years later? Now when Val touched me, it felt like a sickly, slow spreading illness. I felt compelled to retch back from it whenever it was near me for fear it would encapsulate so much of my body that I'd never recover. When Colin touched me, it was like he had the antidote. Whatever of Val's germs still clung to my body were slowly peeled away with each passing moment I spent with his hands on mine. Val was the darkness and Colin was a long awaited dawn.

I'd have to wait hours to see him or my parents, so I'd have to settle for a shower to try and get Val off of me. As I walked down the sunny lane towards my house, I let my mind drift to what I should get Colin for his birthday. He was a difficult person to shop for. He didn't ask for things often, and when he made the mistake of doing so, my parents bought whatever he requested for him on the spot. I considered trying to find another football locket, but the concept seemed tainted now. I was still giving myself mental lashes daily for miscon-struing Colin's behavior and letting it cost us time together. A locket that reminded us of that might not be the best idea, but even as I thought it, I touched the spot on my neck where mine used to hang and wished that it was there. Curse younger me for ending things in as dramatic a fashion as possible. I could have ripped it off and hung onto it at least. It was in a landfill somewhere for sure.

I rounded the corner onto my block and when I looked up at my house, I noticed someone sitting on the front stairs. My heart leapt as I got closer and realized who it was, but my brain was concerned with the reasoning.

"Colin?"

Colin's face shot up and a brilliant smile curved across his jaw. "Hey, beautiful."

My face was warming already. "What are you doing here?"

He blinked plainly at me like it should have been obvious. "Waiting for you."

I bent over and smacked a quick kiss on his forehead. "That's not what I mean." I unlocked the front door and held it open for Colin to walk through. "Shouldn't you be on your way to an away game right now?"

When the door was safely closed, Colin's palms taped to the sides of my neck and pushed me back against it. He dropped his lips to mine, and unlike the trapped and helpless way I felt when Val pushed me against his door, having Colin do it lit me on fire.

"I didn't want to do that," he huffed, not five centimeters from my face. "I wanted to see you."

Joy whipped around me like a torrential wind. "I wanted to see you too."

My arms coiled around Colin's body and took hold on his back. His lips returned to mine, this time armed with his tongue and I twirled us into the living room and down onto the couch. Our noses flicked against one another as we seeded deeper into one another. I was fighting for air in no time. I took my mouth from Colin's for a brief moment.

"If you skip games, you'll get kicked off the team," I warned.

Colin raised an eyebrow. "Is that what you're worried about right now?"

I thought about it. Why was I worried about that right now? "I'm not."

Colin kissed my cheek and then trailed lower. He stamped his lips over the side of my neck and down to my collarbone. When he got to where my shirt interfered with his adventure, he grabbed the edges of it with his hands.

Just as Colin was lifting my shirt over my head,

we heard the sound of simultaneous cars pulling into the driveway. I looked over my shoulder, seeing the shadows of my parents climbing out of their cars through the light blocking curtains in the living room.

I looked back at Colin. "Shouldn't they at least be headed to your away game right now?"

Colin looked like he was ready to kill himself. "They would be if I hadn't responsibly texted them to tell them I was skipping it."

I groaned. "God dammit, Undinger."

Colin chuckled. "I'm sorry." He returned my shirt to its natural position and then we sat up on the couch and put a suspicious amount of space between us. I quickly pulled out my phone and started up some music as if that's what we'd been doing the whole time. Colin looked at me. "I don't want to wait anymore."

"Well, whose fault is that?"

"I'm serious," Colin continued. "Can we finish later?"

My whole body started to tingle wildly. I wanted that too. "If we can sneak down to the basement, we should be okay."

Colin grinned and nodded. "After they go to sleep?"

I was certain if I could see my heart, I'd see it

just bat-shit crazy throwing itself against all the walls in my chest. "After they go to sleep. I'll text you."

Colin sat back against the couch and stared up at the ceiling, a look of excitement and anticipation on his face that gave me chills. "Can't wait."

## 21

## COLIN

Every time I checked the time on my phone, I was certain an hour had passed, but it had only been a couple of minutes. It was after 11, and I was expecting to hear from Tatiana much sooner, but she still hadn't texted me. I didn't want to text her; didn't want to be too eager or desperate, but what was she doing? Had she fallen asleep by accident? Did she forget? Or was she just flat out standing me up?

As the clock ticked towards midnight, I decided I would text her. I picked up my phone and started to type a message, when I saw the three dots on her side of the message feed, indicating she was typing to me. I waited, and eventually a message popped up.

. . .

*Okay. Come Down.*

*On my way.*

It was simple, but it did things to my body I didn't know were possible. There was no reason that less than ten words exchanged between us should be shooting down south and tightening my pants already. I wasn't even downstairs yet. I tried to shake my head free of the excitement so that I didn't seem purely sex-motivated. It was going to be amazing to be with her again, this time with no regrets, but it wasn't just that I was going to get to have her again. It was Tatiana. Finally accepting our relationship to this degree meant that an actual relationship was the next natural step, right? I was that much closer to being able to finally call her mine and mine alone, and that thought shot me above cloud nine to clouds twenty or twenty-one.

I grabbed my backpack and pulled it over my shoulder. It no longer had my books in it, but the whole host of supplies I'd snuck out to buy before dinner. I told the Marquettes I just wanted some fresh air and that I was going to sit at a park and do some homework. None of it was true, and I don't think they believed me, but it didn't matter to me. If I could get out to grab the things I wanted to grab, that's what counted. I snuck out of my room as quietly as I could, tiptoed away from the Marquettes' bedroom at the end of the hallway, and started down the stairs.

The Marquette's home had a completely finished basement that had actually been offered as my bedroom when I first came to live with them. When they presented me with the option to stay down there or in the room across from Tatiana, it was a no-brainer, the closer I could be to her, the better. It had a couch that pulled out into a bizarrely comfortable futon and an entertainment center. It was supposed to be their "home theater," but the Marquettes, Tatiana included, much preferred to snuggle together in their living room and as such, most movie watching happened up there.

I crept down the stairs and when I got to the bottom, I froze in place. Tatiana was standing in front of the futon, which had been pulled out, in the pink kimono she'd bought at the food festival. She'd skipped the sash, probably because she still hadn't figured out how to tie it, but the way it hung loosely around her body with nothing to hold it in place, gave the traditional garb an obscenely erotic appearance. Her black bra and underwear just barely peeked out through an opening in the sides and what blood hadn't flooded into my lower appendage started rushing there with lightning speed. Her hair and makeup had been freshly done and the entire room was filled with the fresh smell of some flowery perfume. Mystery solved of what took so long.

"W-wow." I managed to convince my legs to take a step forward. "I... you... wow."

Tatiana smiled. "Thank you."

I looked down at myself, wearing my same, basic gray sweatpants and black tank top. "I'm underdressed."

Tatiana giggled and it was as sweet as songbirds in the morning. "Don't underestimate the power of gray sweats."

With any luck, they'd be off soon anyway, so it didn't matter much. I wanted to jump right to it, my southern regions definitely cast their votes there, but I had a plan. I hadn't expected Tatiana to come fully armed to that battle, but I wasn't one to be defeated easily.

I put a finger up. "Just one second."

I set my backpack down, unzipped the main

pocket, and started to pull out all of my supplies. I pulled the pack of condoms I'd bought out first. It wasn't the most romantic of the things I'd purchased, but I wanted her to know my head was in the right place. I tossed the condoms onto the bed and then went back in to pull out the rose petals and tea lights next. I scattered the rose petals over the bed and around it, and then set the tea lights up on any surface I could find, clicking them on as I went. I pulled out my bluetooth speaker and phone next, setting them up as close to the futon as I could get them. I navigated to the playlist of songs I'd spent the last two hours carefully picking out. I wanted a perfect soundtrack for our first official time. I kept it on a low volume, I didn't want us to get caught, but I still wanted Tatiana to be able to hear the words of the songs I most associated with her. When everything was set up, I walked over to the basement light and clicked it off, leaving only the tea lights to illuminate the room. The faux flames flickered against Tatiana's caramel skin and it was exactly as I imagined it.

"What is all this?" Tatiana asked.

I walked over to her, threading my arms under the flaps of the kimono and around her warm, satin skin. I pulled her close to me and looked down into her eyes, inviting her to sway gently with me to the music. "This is always how I imagined our first time would be."

Tatiana's eyes shimmered. "I didn't realize you thought about stuff like that. Do you... Do you think about that kind of stuff often? Not just this part, but all the parts?"

I nodded. "Yeah. Every day since you first walked away from me." I saw her expression turn sad and regretted my choice of words. I ducked my head towards hers to pull her into a kiss. I left her lips, but kept my face close. "I think I always hoped we'd find each other again."

Tatiana nodded. "I did too."

We continued to just move to the music. We were in no rush. My fingers trailed along Tatiana's back and her fingers locked into each other behind my neck. She looked into my eyes and if everything had crumbled around us leaving just her and I laced together, I wouldn't have cared. I felt the pressure of her hands against my neck, coaxing me closer, and I didn't resist. She pressed our lips together and I took a drink of her happily. She leaned towards the bed and I followed her lead, dropping down onto it. We continued to kiss, each moment growing in heat and intensity. I rolled her so she was on her back, and the Kimono drifted open and laid around her like a perfectly wrapped present falling open.

I lifted my own shirt up and over my head and found myself stuck staring at Tatiana below me. Artwork that pristine was typically reserved for the fanciest of museums. I couldn't help but think that I was finally being repaid for all of the misfortune I'd had to endure. Tatiana's barely clothed form, her chocolate eyes sunk deeply into my own, begging me to keep going. That was one hell of a reward for waiting. I fell back over her, finding a place on her neck to appreciate. I tried to keep it low, but the way I settled there, licking and nibbling at the spot, it was going to leave a mark.

Tatiana's slender fingers crawled into my hair and found a spot on my head that she'd somehow turned into something of a hotspot for me. It sent jolts of electricity shooting through me. I moved on her from her neck, continuing lower. Her chest was a canvas, clean to be painted by me. I moved my lips along any place that they could reach. My hands were already moving on impulse to the front clasp of Tatiana's bra. It parted the cups from each other, and when the fabric dropped away from her, I had to close my eyes and take a breath.

Didn't I see her breasts the other time? Why did everything feel so fresh and new?

Tatiana rubbed my head. "Is everything okay?"

My head shot up. I slunk back up to hover over her face. "Yeah, you're just so beautiful I can't keep my composure."

She kissed me quickly. "Why do you have to keep it?" All of the parts of me that had been clamoring in all different directions stopped and focused on Tatiana's innocently curious question. "I'm here for you, aren't I? If you want to let go, let go."

It snapped me into alignment. Of course. I'd spent all of the past five years holding myself back. Stealing quick glances at school when it was safe, never saying too much about our past, even in the past couple of weeks, just going only so far. I didn't have to anymore. I touched my lips to Tatiana and my hands found the perfect mounds I'd just set free. Her sweet musing opened the floodgates. Hopefully she wouldn't come to regret it.

I leaned away from Tatiana just enough to hook my fingers into the hem of her underwear and pull them free of her legs. I looked her over and she grinned at me. "If you keep looking at me like that, I'm gonna get a big ego."

"You should already have one."

I worked my own pants and boxers off, discarding them on the floor, and sat with my back against the back of the couch that served as a headboard when it was in its bed form. I held my arms out to Tatiana and she didn't hesitate. She sat up and straddled her legs on either side of me and situated herself in my lap. I took delightful handfuls of her backside as she kissed me again, letting her tongue swirl around with mine. I grabbed the pack of condoms next to me and took one from the box. My heart pounded as I covered myself, preparing to be with Tatiana, for what felt like the first time. I'd been with another woman before, and even Tatiana, but this was so profoundly different from anything before. This was truly my first time, with someone I loved, someone who loved me. I would remember it forever.

All of our actions started to blend into one another. Her casual movements, positioning herself in the way I needed her to be for access, which I didn't wait another moment to pass through. She rose and fell, drowning me in a pool that was somehow as hot as a blazing bonfire. I tasted her breasts and the sultry sounds that spilled out of her would be my nightsong for years to come.

My hands were endlessly unsatisfied. They travelled to every corner and crevasse, sometimes squeezing, sometimes just softly walking across the skin, all working to figure out which movements caused different reactions from the goddess on top of me. I did my best to commit to memory the way she had her head tossed back and her lips carelessly parted. I kissed her shoulder and made a decision to venture into a small experiment. I bit down on the spot, hard. Not so hard that I thought it would hurt her, but more than a nip. Simultaneous with my chomp, Tatiana squeezed around me and it was almost as if I was going to burst into dust. If someone had asked me to spell my name in that moment I would have failed.

"Shh." Tatiana pulled me into a kiss.

Did I make a noise? I didn't even realize. Her movements changed to a sublime way that moved me in new directions. I was an innocent young man losing his virginity to a cruel succubus. She was taking the very color from my body and I was perfectly pleased to let her. When she took her lips away from mine, our eyes locked into each other, and then she started to go faster. Her hands snaked around my neck and up into the base of my hair, and my arms wrapped around her body and pulled her as close to me as I could get her. I was certain the magic of the moment was going to lift the furniture around us off the ground and send it swirling about the room. It wasn't just my nether regions galloping towards the edge of the cliff, it was all of me, like an army of men storming towards the horizon not realizing it was actually a steep drop off.

"I love you." The words left my mouth with no prior consideration. My love for Tatiana wasn't a conscious thing anymore. It was as much a part of me as the absent-minded blinks of my eyes. It wasn't something I knew, it was something I breathed. Most people needed food and water to live, but I needed Tatiana. As long as I had her, nothing else mattered.

Tatiana's head nodded weakly as she whimpered on top of me. She was shaking and swerving and moaning and I could sense she was as close as I was. "I love you too."

My animal instincts punched my logical self out of the control seat of my body and took over. With a tight hold on Tatiana, I flipped her over to her back, and blanketed myself over her. Like a tide crashing into the shore, I took Tatiana and her voice heightened to the point that now it was me who needed to bring our volume down. I closed my mouth over hers, which only stifled her noises as much as my mouth could hold. I growled against her lips and cursed my body for not being able to hang on more. The horses we were on stormed towards one another, both of our lances out. Neither of us stayed on the saddle. We hooked into each other and both went spilling off our steeds in a blinding and deafening tumble of pleasure. The fall was almost sweeter than the ride. It bounced all around me like a loose superball, causing the hairs on the back of my neck to stand on end and my mouth to go dry.

I went limp against Tatiana, dropping my head to rest above her beautiful breasts. Her chest rose and fell under me and even through the sweat that covered both of our bodies, I felt the cleanest I'd ever been. Tatiana pet my head absently, and I felt my eyes flutter. I could have fallen asleep right there, but I fought through it, I didn't want to be done with the night, not just yet. I pecked her skin a few times just to remind myself that I could. She was in my arms and I never wanted to let her go.

"I'm sorry," Tatiana whispered softly after a long time, and it terrified me to my core. I lifted my head to look into her eyes, and there were tears sliding out of them. "I'm sorry I cost us this. We should have been together a long time ago."

I let out a sigh of relief. I rubbed a hand over her face, swiping the tears away. "All that matters is that we're here now."

She nodded. "I love you."

I could have died a happy man. "I love you."

We shifted around until I was leaning back

against the back of the couch, and Tatiana was nestled between my legs. As beautiful as she looked in her Kimono, I pulled it from around her and draped it over the edge of the bed so that I could take in her true, naked visage. I wrapped my arms around her body and she dropped her head back against my shoulder. I kissed her forehead. How long could we stay like that until we had to get dressed and sneak back up to our bedrooms? How much time was I allotted in that personal heaven?

Tatiana touched a spot on her collarbone and I titled my head. "You do that a lot."

"Hm?" She glanced up at me.

"Touch your chest right there."

"Oh, yeah…" she said, a streak of sadness in her words. "I've done it ever since I got rid of the locket. I wish I hadn't."

I untangled myself from Tatiana. I didn't want to move at all, but it was worth it. I grabbed my backpack and pulled it up onto the bed. I sifted through the front pocket until I found what I was looking for and pulled it out. I dangled Tatiana's half of the locket in front of her and her eyes started to glisten with tears.

"Oh my god." She held out her hand and I dropped it in. "Where… How?"

"When you threw it down, I grabbed it and

took it home. I don't know," I kissed Tatiana's cheek, "I guess I still thought it was important and wanted to keep it."

"Where's your half?"

I reached back into my bag and pulled out my football gloves. I tipped back the fabric that typically wrapped around my wrist, where I'd glued in my half of the locket. "I never stopped thinking about you, Tatiana. Not for a second."

Tatiana was struggling to find words. Finally, she handed the necklace over and then turned her pristine, bare back to me and took her hair up in her hands. I laced the necklace around her neck and clasped it. Tatiana touched the spot gently and a glowing smile found her face. She turned to face me fully, grabbed my face, and pulled it down to hers. She slid backwards on the bed, taking me with her. Her hands trailed over my back and excitement fled south in anticipation of round two.

## 22

# TATIANA

Seeing Colin in the kitchen the next morning blanketed me in happiness. It wasn't just the love making that came flooding back into my brain, but laying with him, talking with him, and just being with him. He looked up from his cereal and gave me a huge, bright smile. He was so good-looking. His hair was pulled back behind his head, but it didn't matter. Colin looked good anyway he decided to show up. I could see the touch of exhaustion behind his eyes, the same that I assume mine held. We'd gone at it until the early hours of the morning, and thank god I woke up early after drifting off in his arms, otherwise my parents would have gotten quite the shock when they went looking for us after we didn't show up for breakfast. My parents would be beyond pleased to learn that we were together when we were finally ready to tell them so, but I doubted they would be as excited to find out we had sex in their basement with them two floors up, least of all my dad. Beneath his teddy bear facade was an overprotective man who could easily come to dislike Colin if he felt like he was being disrespectful.

"Good morning," I greeted as I walked into the kitchen. I wanted to kiss Colin on sight, but that would have to wait.

Colin watched me as I walked over and sat down in the barstool next to him. "Good morning."

I stared into Colin's green eyes until I could feel my parents gaze on us. I looked over at my mom and her eyebrows were so high I thought they were going to fall off her face. "What?" I asked.

She crossed her arms. "You look nice."

I looked down at my outfit. I'd dug out one of my teal, thin hoodies from the back of my closet and a pair of light blue, acid wash jeans. I suppose it probably was the brightest thing I'd worn in a long time. "Thanks."

She reached across the kitchen island and lifted the half a football locket with a finger. "Where'd you get this?"

I side-glanced Colin and he shrugged. I looked back at my mom. "Colin gave it to me."

Colin held up a hand. "Correction. I just gave it *back* to her."

My mom examined it a little closer in the wake of Colin's clarification. "This is the football necklace you bought forever ago, right?"

I nodded. "Yeah."

My dad tilted his head. "Huh. I guess it didn't even occur to me that we never saw it again after that first day you wore it. How'd you end up with it, Colin?"

"She dropped it and I picked it up," he replied, telling a half-truth. "I didn't really have a good opportunity to give it back to her until recently."

My mom chuckled. "You're the one whose birthday is coming up. You should be getting presents, not giving them."

I was reminded that I never did decide what I was going to get Colin for his birthday. My mom was right, what he'd given me was so special, that it elevated what I wanted to give him in return. He deserved something really wonderful, but we were still getting to know the people we'd grown into. I didn't really know what he would like.

"You two walking to school again?" My dad asked.

"Yeah." Colin finished off his cereal and my mom scooped up the bowl before he could stand to try and put it in the dishwasher himself. "If that's okay?"

My dad beamed. "Of course. It'll probably be too cold soon to do it anyway. Enjoy it while you can."

I ate a quick breakfast of a banana and toast and then Colin and I left for school. We had barely cleared the threshold of my front door and Colin had interlocked his hand with mine. If I knew my parents, and I was pretty sure I did, they had their noses pressed to the glass of the front living room window, watching as we walked away. It didn't bother me. They loved Colin just as much as I did. If anything, they were relieved.

We walked slowly on purpose. There was no need to rush and neither of us wanted to. Until I had ended things with Val, my relationship with Colin was pretty much pigeonholed to our walks to and from school.

"Hey." I don't know why it felt weird breaking our blissful silence. "What do you want for your birthday?"

A loud laugh flew out of him. "Because last night wasn't enough?"

"No. You can have that whenever. That's not a

present." The words ran out of me before I realized the magnitude of what I said. A quick glance at Colin proved that the concept had not been lost on him. "What?"

"Really? I can?" he asked.

I shrugged. "Obviously."

We were skating around what we hadn't done before; made our relationship official. "I mean, I don't want to do anything else while I'm still with Val. Not so much for him, but for you, I..." I swallowed hard. "I want you to be the only one." Not that I had any plans to sleep with Val ever again, Colin pretty much was the only one already.

"That's what I want." Colin stopped and turned to face me. "For my birthday. I want to be the only one."

"That's the plan," I murmured and Colin shook his head.

"No, I don't want it to be 'The plan,' anymore." He was looking at me with a brand new expression I'd never seen before. It lingered somewhere between longing and needing. "I want to be together. Right now. For real. I don't want to wait anymore."

I had already planned on ending things with Val on Sunday, but I didn't tell Colin that. I knew if he knew my plans he'd try to interfere. I wanted to handle things myself. "I don't either."

"Well then what are you waiting for?" he asked.

I thought of how much it freaked me out when I tried to break up with Val the day before. He was growing increasingly more possessive and aggressive when it came to me. My idea to try again in the full view of the public eye was fool-proof I hoped. Colin must have picked up on my fear, because he lifted my hand to his lips and dropped a quick kiss on each of my knuckles. "If you're afraid, I'll help you. If he's still threatening you, we could tell Coach Nash or Mr. Devine."

"No!" I barked and Colin recoiled a bit. I dropped my head. "I'm sorry, I just… Those rumors were bad enough. I don't want anyone else to know." I looked back up at him. "He's been weird lately, but I don't think he'll hurt me. I promise, I'll end things. Soon, just give me a little more time."

Colin sighed. "I've waited this long."

I went up on my toes to kiss his lips. "I love you. I want to be with you too. More than anything." My words seemed to help.

We shared one final kiss before putting a more natural distance between us to walk into school. It didn't stop people from staring at us as we moved, but I was much less concerned about them, and much more concerned with Val. I waved goodbye to Colin as he left for the senior wing, and then I went and found Billy. He was already standing near my locker and when he noticed me walking, an expression of impressed shock lit up over his face.

"Wow. A primary color? Are we about to be smited?" he asked.

"Shut up," I hissed. "And it's not a primary color."

"It's blue."

"It's *teal.*"

Billy fake gagged. "It's blue."

I put my backpack and jacket away, grabbed my books for my first class, and then linked my arm in Billy's and pulled him towards a set of tables and chairs that each of the wings had for studying and general lounging before, between, and after classes. We went to the one furthest back and sat down.

"Colin and I had sex last night."

Billy's jaw dropped. "YES!"

"Shhhhhh!" I laughed at him. "Jesus, do you *have* another volume."

"What happened?" Billy asked, leaning in.

"Sex," I replied, confused.

"No." Billy waved his hand through the air. "What *happened?*"

"Oh. I got home after school yesterday and he was there instead of going to his away game and he said he skipped because he wanted to see me. We kissed, made out, yada yada, and then my parents came home."

Billy shook his head. "Cock blockers."

"Tell me about it." I snickered at the very obscure and uncomfortable description of my parents. "Anyway. Colin said he didn't want to wait anymore, and I didn't either, so that night we snuck down to the basement. It was so beautiful, he went out and got rose petals and tea lights and scattered them everywhere, and he'd made this playlist just for us."

"Well done," Billy threw in quickly.

"And it just happened…" I got coy. "And then it happened again."

Billy started to laugh. "I feel like I need to bro-out with him about it."

"Yeah, that won't be weird at *all*." I pulled a piece of paper out of one of my notebooks and wrote Colin's number on it and handed it to Billy. "This is his number."

Billy was taken aback. "I was just kidding about bro-ing out."

"I know. This is just in case. I'm going to break up with Val on Sunday. I'm going to meet him at a public place and just tell him honestly that my feelings aren't there anymore. I'm going to try my best to let him down gently and hopefully everything will be okay, but just in case." I put my hand on the paper. "If you don't hear from me by noon, call Colin."

## 23

## COLIN

I was truly happy. The sun was setting on the Marquettes' beautifully decorated backyard, covered in balloons, streamers, and giant '18' cutouts. A picnic table was overflowing with delicious food, all my mom's recipes that Cristiano had recreated from scratch, and in the middle was a massive, orange and black colored, two-tier cake that Kya and Tatiana had baked together. A card table with an orange table cloth was piled high with presents wrapped in every variety of color and pattern imaginable and my aunt, Coach Nash, all the seniors from my football team, a few of my parents' employees from the restaurant, Tatiana, and her parents were standing around me with smiles on their faces. I couldn't help but feel like my parents were there too. If they'd planned something for my birthday, it probably would have been something pretty similar; homemade food and the people I loved most--perfect.

"Did you have fun?" Tatiana asked as we stood in the driveway waving goodbye to all my guests.

"I really did." I put my arm around her shoulders and placed a gentle kiss on her forehead. "Thank you."

For the first time in a very long time, I was totally at peace. The relaxation that was settling over my body made it weary, desperate to put a completion stamp on this day. I yawned and Tatiana chuckled. "You look tired."

"I've been sleeping better lately, but it just reminds me how shittily I was sleeping before. I'm still catching up."

Tatiana patted my stomach a few times like an owner cuddling its cat. "Go lay down. I'm gonna help my parents clean up, then I'll be headed to bed myself."

"Can I come lay with you?" I squeezed her closer to me, not wanting to let her go.

An already present grin grew into a large smile. "I'd like that." She glanced around and then stood up on the tips of her toes to kiss me before walking back across the front yard towards the gate in the back. "I'll text you," she called out before disappearing around the house.

I took the box of my presents that Kya had packed up and carried it upstairs to my room. My parents would have been thrilled with the spread. A new set of pads from my coach and players and the complete set of the latest edition of a graphic novel series I enjoyed from my aunt. Kya, Cristiano, and Tatiana had come up with a hairbrained idea to buy me 18 gifts, one for each year of my life. They got me a few new articles of clothing, a new pair of cleats for football, a TV and gaming system for my bedroom, a new backpack (though that was mostly for Tatiana who abhorred the falling apart one I was perfectly content to continue carrying around), a large supply of some of my favorite colognes and hair products, and topped it all off with tickets to the Bahamas; a family vacation we would take over the summer. I would have been happy just to spend the time with the people I cared about, but the gifts were all so thoughtful that I was overflowing with joy.

I pulled out the gaming system and TV and started to set them up in my room when my phone buzzed with a text.

.  .  .

*I'm here, whenever you're
ready.*

*I'm always ready for you.*

I stopped what I was doing and walked across the hall to Tatiana's room. I entered and she was leaning against her headboard flipping through her phone, already in a pair of shorts and one of my t-shirts. "I've been looking for that," I grumbled playfully.

"I know. I didn't tell you that I had it because I didn't want to give it back." Tatiana flashed a mischievous grin at me, and it shot south. I understood her desire not to want to sleep together again until after she'd ended things with Val, but god I hated it.

Still, as I crawled into her bed, laying my head in her lap and instantly earning myself her fingers gliding into my hair to rub my head gently, I was happy just to be near her. I pulled out my phone and started to scroll through mine as well. We stayed that way in silence for a while, just enjoying being in the same space. Things had always been that way between Tatiana and I, maybe even when we were pretending to hate each other. I always felt better walking into the lunch room and being flipped off by her before sitting down at a table to eat, and it always seemed like she was glowering when she walked into school, but once we'd crossed paths, she seemed in a lighter mood with Billy next time I saw her. For us, the nearer we were to each other, the better off we were.

Tatiana let out a sigh a bit later and I looked up at her. "What's up?"

"Oh, nothing. I'm just so comfortable. I want to fall asleep."

I shrugged. "Well, I think that's okay."

She chuckled at me. "I know, but if we both fall asleep and my parents catch us, it wouldn't be good." Then she groaned. "Even though I'm pretty sure they already know."

"They do keep giving us those satisfied smiles," I added. "Do you think they'd really be mad if they caught us?"

"Oh don't get me wrong. They're going to be *thrilled* that we're together. Over the moon, but unless you want my dad on you like bees on honey, at least kind of pretending we aren't is probably in our best interest," Tatiana replied. "He'll be a happy bee though."

"I can't wait to tell them."

Tatiana looked down at me. "Really?"

I nodded. "Yeah. I remember back when I first kissed you, I told my parents the second you got out of the car. My mom asked me what I wanted for dinner and I blurted out 'I kissed Tatiana.'" I laughed remembering the way my dad swerved the car twisting his head around like an owl to look at me when I said it. "My mom just started clapping."

"You told your parents? I didn't know that." Tatiana's expression was a mix of curiosity and sadness. "Were they really that excited?"

"Yeah, I mean... They loved you Tati. It's the same with your parents how you think they're gonna be excited. My folks wanted you as a daughter almost more than they wanted me as a son."

Tatiana went silent and I repositioned to take her into my arms. "What?"

She sniffled. "Because of me, they never got to see it." She pulled her knees up to her head and I held her close. My own eyes were starting to blur in the wake of the sentence. "I'm sorry."

"We both played a part." I rubbed her back. "Besides, I know this sounds cheesy, but they know. They can see it." Tatiana's shoulders started to rise and fall more dramatically and I thought she was sobbing, but then her head lifted and she was laughing. "What?" I asked.

Her eyes widened. "I hope they can't see *all* of it."

"Pfft." I laughed alongside her imagining the couple of times we'd had sex, and whole host of times we'd made out. "You and me both, baby."

Tatiana slid down a little bit so she could lay her head against my chest. "I hope they know how much I love their son."

My heart exploded. "They do. I tell them."

"What other stuff do you tell them?" Tatiana asked, her hands moving to play with the base of my shirt.

That was a loaded question. I'd taken to talking to my parents urns that sat on the dresser by my bed. At first I just told them that I missed them and wished they were back, but as time dragged on, I started to tell them everything, just like I had when they were living. "I tell them about my days. I tell them that their friends are taking good care of me. I tell them how football is going and about my plans for college."

I felt Tatiana tense beneath my arms. "College…"

"Yeah…" We hadn't breached the subject. Tatiana was still only a junior, so there was another year before she would graduate. At first, I'd exclusively considered colleges that took me out of Colorado, but in the past few weeks, I'd been looking at local options. "I've been thinking about Mesa lately."

Tatiana's head whipped up to look at me. "Colorado Mesa? That's so close."

I laughed. "I know. I need someplace close. I still have all of my parents' affairs to take care of, and that's going to take a while. Besides, you'll be here. We have a whole year after I graduate before we could move in together or something."

Tatiana's cheeks instantly got two shades darker. "Move in?"

"Well yeah, Tati. I mean, I assumed we'd live together eventually. That is, if you wanted to?"

She nodded. "I do!"

I laughed. "Oh, good. I was afraid there for a second."

She grinned. "I wish we didn't have to wait."

I kissed her on the top of her head. "I know, me too." I could feel a touch of restlessness settling over us, so I pulled out my phone and held it out in front of us. "Should we look for a place?"

Tatiana smiled. "Right now?"

"Yeah. We don't have to make the decision right now, but I plan to move sooner rather than later anyway. Especially if you're thinking we won't be able to have sex here because," I scoffed, "that shit is *not* going to work for me."

Tatiana started laughing and it made me happy to know I was improving her mood. "Me either."

We spent the next couple of hours looking through different apartment listings between Orchard Mesa and Grand Junction. We were picking out the things we definitely wanted and definitely didn't want, and Tatiana even started to use a model decorating app to play around with how we'd appoint our place. That led to window shopping furniture, and I was already developing an idea in my head of decorating an apartment one day and then inviting Tatiana over to surprise her. Maybe for an anniversary.

When would our anniversary be? The day we first kissed a few weeks ago? The day we first kissed five years ago? The day we first had sex? The night when we had the first sex that we both counted?

"Hey, Tati. Here's a question." I waited for a response, but heard nothing. "Tati."

I looked over at her face, and her eyes were closed and she was breathing in and out deeply. *Yeah. That's not important right now. We'll figure it out later.*

I kissed her on top of her head once again, and

then pulled her blanket over us and clicked off her lamp. I knew she was concerned about getting caught, but it didn't bother me as much. If it meant I could fall asleep next to Tatiana, I was willing to risk it.

## 24

## TATIANA

Waking up with Colin wrapped around me made getting out of bed even more difficult. Sundays were typically lazy in our household, so my parents probably hadn't discovered Colin sleeping in my bed instead of his own, but even if they had, they didn't bother us, which I was grateful for. I crawled out of bed as quietly as I could, my feet hitting the floor feeling like passing through my own personal heaven into my own personal hell. It was time to go and deal with Val.

I'd already decided that my outfit for the day was going to be modest. It wasn't as if it mattered much, Val's and my relationship started during the thick of my days of only wearing hoodies and loose jeans, but I still didn't want to exacerbate an already painful situation by looking my best when I did it. I was hoping that if I was showing as little skin as possible, had my hair up in a messy bun, and was wearing my glasses as a rare choice over my contacts, Val would be relieved to be parting from a swamp rat. Anything I could do to stack the odds in my favor. I selected an all black hoodie and a pair of dark blue jeans that fit me loosely and flared at the bottom, opted not to put any makeup on, and pushed my phone and wallet into my pocket instead of going for a full purse.

I grabbed a piece of notebook paper and wrote Colin a note to find when he woke up. I didn't want to get too into the details, I knew he would try and interfere if he knew where I was going or what I was doing, but I wanted to give him a little hope that his waiting was nearly over.

*Colin,*

> *I'm going to spend some time with Billy this morning.*
> *We're going to grab your birthday present.*
> *Keep it between us, okay?*
> *I love you.*

*--Tati*

I folded the note, wrote Colin's name on the front, and set it on my bedside table, on top of his phone so he was sure to see it.

I opened the door as quietly as I could and slunk out into the hallway, closing it behind me just as softly. I was disappointed to see my parents' bedroom door open. If it were closed, it would indicate they were still asleep inside and I could leave the house undetected, but they were both early risers. I walked down the stairs and into the kitchen where they were sharing a pleasant conversation over breakfast.

My mom frowned when she saw me. "That's so dark."

I understood the frustration. I'd been getting back to my old palette as of late, mixing lots of color into my wardrobe and wearing my hair down more often; I probably looked more like my stale, depressed self.

"I know. I was feeling lazy," I lied. "I'm going to go do some shopping with Billy. I need some clothes that protect me from the cold but don't also make me look like I'm on a constant stealth mission."

That seemed to brighten my mom a little. "Oh. Good."

"It's so early." My dad looked down at his watch. "Will stores even be open?"

"We're going to get breakfast first." Unfortunately, lying came second nature to me. I'd had to do a lot of it in the past year since I started seeing Val. "Then shopping."

"Oh." My dad smiled. "Do you need any money?"

I shook my head. "I'm still living off of mom's random generosity of a few weeks ago. Thanks though." I turned around, tossing my hand through the air. "See you later."

"Bye baby," my mom called after me. "Love you."

"Love you guys too." I slipped on a pair of my understated tennis shoes and walked out the front door.

The morning was already colder than I was expecting it to be. Fall was in full effect with Winter nipping at its heels. If I was actually hanging out with Billy, I'd be climbing into his car, but I planned to walk to the diner where I was meeting Val for breakfast so that I didn't have to be alone with him. Val was after sex only, that was clear, but I'd managed to convince him that we needed breakfast for 'fuel' before a day of debauchery. Given that it was clear he quickly lost faith I was going to see him at all by the way he constantly confirmed meeting up via text message, when I doubled down on wanting to see him so long as we could get breakfast first, he obliged happily.

It was a brisk twenty minute walk to the edge-of-downtown street where the diner was. I took the opportunity to text Billy and tell him I was en route and he warned me to be careful. I promised to text him as soon as I was done and he made sure to warn me to text if it's going to be longer than I'm thinking. He's not waiting until 12:01 or 12:02. If he hasn't heard from me by noon on the nose, he's calling Colin. I told him I understood.

The diner was one of those mom and pop seeming places that was actually a chain. It had neon booth seats that were ripped on purpose and tables with the menus laid right into the table. There were enough patrons inside that I felt comfortable I'd be safe from anything Val may try to pull, but even as I sat, it felt more like trying to just get through a regular breakup. Val had been strange lately, I couldn't deny that, and at times he'd been forceful with me, but I'd gotten nasty in the wake of Colin's and my mixup. I understood all too well how love can make a person act outside of character. I'd spent almost a year with Val and he'd never been like that before. I was confident he wouldn't hurt me or do anything too crazy. I just had to let him down easy and get back to Colin and on with the rest of our lives. I took the few final minutes before Val arrived to text Billy.

*I made it to the diner.*

*Oh my god. Okay. Please be so careful. Text me when you're done.*

*I will, I promise.*

*You need to text me if it takes longer too. I'm not waiting until 12:01 or 12:02. If I haven't heard from you at noon on the nose, I'm calling Colin.*

*I will, but it's okay. I really don't think Val will hurt me.*

*I sure hope you're right, Tati. I can't go to jail for killing a teacher, especially when Colin and your parents will be right there next to me.*

*Lol. I'll be okay. Talk
to you soon.*

"Hey beautiful." I looked over my shoulder and Val was reaching the booth I'd picked out. We'd pretty much decided we would never kiss or act romantic towards one another in public, but when he passed me, he leaned down and kissed the top of my head. "I'm glad to see you."

"Hi," I greeted, not wanting to tell any additional lies.

"How are you?" he asked.

I nodded. "I'm pretty good." His eyes scanned me up and down for the first time. Had I made a mistake dressing down? "What?" I asked.

He shook his head. "Nothing. Just reminding myself how stunning you are. Even for being so simply dressed." That was sweet.

Val was charming and charismatic on top of being good looking. I wanted to be with Colin, and compared to him, Val was no contest, but something about Val's presence was a jedi mind trick. I felt a tiny impulse to bail, enjoy breakfast, and let him take me home.

I took a breath and cleared my throat. If I

didn't get this over with soon, I was going to chicken-out the same way I had in his class a few days ago. "Look. There's no easy way to do this--"

Val closed his eyes and bowed his head. "I knew it."

I should have known it wouldn't be easy. "Val." He looked up at me, and to my shock, his eyes were gathering moisture in the corners. "I'm sorry."

"It's Colin Undinger isn't it?" he asked. "You *are* sleeping with him."

I didn't want to lie, but he didn't need to know the gory details. "I am in love with Colin. I always have been, since we were kids. I thought he was out of my life for good, but these past several weeks with him living with us have shown me that door isn't closed."

"When you said you loved me, did you mean it?"

No. "I did." I didn't. "I mean… I think I loved you based on my understanding of love at that time. I'm sorry. I know that doesn't sound fair, but I've learned a lot about myself in a very short period of time. You've helped me grow as a person, and maybe if the circumstances hadn't become what they did, you and I would…" I was going down a bad road. "I'm sorry."

Val sat back in his booth. He looked around. "I

could use some water. Why hasn't the waitress come over?"

I pushed my glass towards him. "I asked her not to. Said I had to deliver some bad news."

He grabbed it and drank it all the way down until nothing but the ice was left. "Wow."

I didn't quite know where to go next. I didn't feel like I'd reached the end of the level yet, but I wasn't sure how to clear the next obstacle. I couldn't just get up and walk away, it was only right to make sure he was okay before leaving. "Are you okay?"

He looked at me. "No, I'm not okay. I really *do* love you. Not by some fractured standard, but by the whole thing."

"I know. It's because you're a wonderful man, and someday you're going to be with someone who will love you by that same standard, and that woman will be very lucky." I felt compelled to reach out and take his hand, but resisted.

Val stared down at the table. "I can't say I'm not disappointed, Tati. I was considering quitting so that you being my student wouldn't be a hindrance for us." He looked up again. "If it's that, we can work through that."

I shook my head. "It was never that."

That seemed to hit him hard. "Oh." He took a

deep breath and then looked into my eyes. He looked devastated and it hurt, but breakups weren't supposed to feel good. "I understand. I just want you to be happy."

That took me back a step. It was unexpected. "Really?" I shouldn't have asked, but the word skipped out of me before I could stop it.

He chuckled. "Of course. A woman as great as you? I just want you to have everything you've ever wanted."

He was turning on the charm again, but I was over the hill now. I just had to stay strong a little bit longer. "Thank you. I want that for you too."

He cast a playful roll of his eyes. "Well, not everything I want, because…" He motioned to me.

*Duh, Tatiana.* "Right. Sorry."

"That's okay." He nodded as if he was finally accepting what was happening. "Well, I guess that's it, huh?"

"Do you need a ride home?" he asked.

I shook my head. He was taking it oddly well for how bizarre he'd been behaving, but I didn't want to take any unnecessary risks. It'd be just as cold a walk home as it was a walk there, but then I'd be able to crawl back into Colin's warm and waiting arms, tell him we could finally be together for good, and put all of the muck of the past five years behind me.

"I'm okay. I like the walk."

He nodded. "Yeah. A whole car ride with your ex wouldn't be comfy. I get it."

"Thank you for everything, Val," I finished. "I'll go."

I stood up, taking one final look at Val's frame, slumped and defeated against the neon blue diner seat, and then turned around and left. When the cold air hit my face again, I took a deep inhale of it, smelling the sweet autumn leaves mingle with the smells from the diner. I'd have to come up with some excuse why shopping didn't work out, but I had a whole twenty minute walk to figure it out.

I pulled out my phone and shot Billy a quick text that I was done and it went better than expected and I was headed home. He was relieved and promised to call me later after running errands with his mom to get the details. I pulled out my headphones and was setting them into my ears when I felt something slam against my head, rocking it with a searing sting. I flew forward, my phone flinging out of my hand onto the concrete as I landed hard on the sidewalk. I groaned as I rolled over to investigate and Val was standing over me with a huge stick in his hand.

His image looming over me blurred and shaked from my daze, but I could see that his eyes were wild and frantic. An evil smile bled across his face. "I told you already, you're mine."

The last thing I saw was him lifting the stick above his head and bringing it down again before completely blacking out.

## 25

## COLIN

I felt unsettled. It was almost 4:00pm and Tatiana still hadn't come home. She left me a note saying that she was going shopping with Billy for my birthday present, but the only gift we'd discussed her getting me was ending things with Val. If she was with Billy, I had to assume she was okay, but the idea of her being around Val made me nervous. She'd been tight-lipped about it, but it was obvious Val had been threatening her more recently. She looked terrified whenever she had to go and see him and I knew that was what was keeping her from breaking up with him sooner. I wished she'd let me go with her; hell if I knew where they were I'd go myself.

I tried calling and texting Tatiana several times,

but she hadn't responded so I'd spent the last hour trying and failing to find Billy on social media. He was an odd duck, so I assumed he was probably listed under a pseudonym, which was his prerogative, but it was annoying as shit when I was trying to get in touch with him.

A knock on my door dragged me up from my phone and by the time I'd looked up, Kya was standing in the doorway and Cristiano was already a few feet in. It felt like a bad omen. They never entered without making sure it was okay.

"Hi." I could tell on both their faces that they were perturbed and it scared me. "What's going on?"

"Do you know where Tatiana is?" Cristano asked.

I looked over at the note on my dresser. "She told me she was going shopping with Billy." I looked back up at them and that didn't appear to be the answer they were looking for.

Kya already looked on the verge of tears. "That's what she told us too, but we just saw Billy with his mother getting into the car at the grocery store."

My heart fell like a lead brick into my stomach. She'd gone to see Val, and she went alone. "What?"

"Do you have any way to get in touch with Billy?" Cristiano asked.

"Yeah." It was a lie, but I had a hail-mary that I was hoping would work. "You guys head downstairs and take a breather. I'm sure she's okay. I'll call Billy right now." I wanted more than anything to be right, but I had a deadly suspicion that I wasn't.

Cristiano turned and took Kya by the hand. "Come on. I'm sure he's right."

As they walked away, I regretted lying. I should have told them what I knew, but if they'd mistaken something and Tatiana really was fine, I didn't want to panic them or make things hard for Tatiana.

I closed the bedroom door again and then called Coach Nash. He was an administrator at school, the counselor no less, so he had to have access to student records.

"Hey Undinger, is everything okay? You never call on Sundays?"

"No." My heart was pounding and sweat was pooling around my head. "I need you to get Billy Benton's number for me."

He groaned. "Listen, kid, I like ya, but I can't just go giving out student information. I could--"

"I think Tatiana went to break up with Val and she went by herself," I blurted out. "She left early this morning and isn't responding to anyone's calls or texts. She told me and her parents she was going to hang out with Billy, but they just saw him at the grocery store with his mom."

"Fuck." Coach Nash let out a huge, heavy sigh. "Alright, give me five minutes, I'll text you."

"Thank you."

I hung up my phone, and as promised, Billy's number came a few seconds later. I clicked it and sent a text.

*Hey, it's Colin Undinger*
*Is Tatiana with you?*

My phone was ringing in my hand a few seconds later; it was Billy. "Hello?"

"Is Tatiana not home?" His voice was an octave higher than normal and distraught.

"No, she told us she was going shopping with you."

Billy's breathing picked up speed. "Oh my god. Oh my god. Oh my god."

It was horrifying me. "What? What's wrong?"

"Tatiana went to go break up with Val this

morning. She met him at a diner, a public place to be safe, and then she sent me a text at like 9 telling me it was done and she was headed home."

"Nine this morning?!" My whole life was flashing before my eyes. Her beautiful smile, the touch of her hands on my skin, her joyous laugh. "Where is she?!"

"I don't know!" Billy was next to hyperventilating on the other end of the phone. "Oh my god. You have to go tell her parents. You have to call the police."

"Do you know where she was meeting him?"

"Yes! I'll text it to you."

I didn't respond and just hung up the phone. I jumped up and bolted down the stairs and Kya and Cristiano must have sensed the urgency in my movements because they were already rushing to the bottom of the stairs when I was clamoring down them.

Kya already had tears streaming down her face. She could see the panic in mine. "I'm sorry. I'm so sorry," I started, my own emotions welling up.

Kya cupped her hands over her mouth and Cristiano pulled on my shoulders. "What is it? Where is she?" His normally even and calm tone was frantic now.

I hated that I had to let the Marquettes down

after everything they'd done for me. "Tatiana." I dropped my head. "Tatiana has been dating one of the teachers at school for like the past year. She was going to break up with him to be with me and she went this morning alone."

Kya went rushing into the kitchen and I could hear her throwing up a moment later. Cristiano shook his head. "Why would you let her go?"

"I didn't know!" Where was my beautiful Tatiana? Was she in danger? "I thought she was with Billy!"

My phone buzzed and an address popped up. I ran around Cristiano into the kitchen and sifted through the drunk drawer for a notepad and pen. I scribbled down the address and forced it against Kya's chest. "This is where she went to meet him. Call the police."

I ran back towards the door, but Cristiano grabbed my arm. "You can't go! She's already in danger, we can't risk you too."

"I have to find her!" Tears started to fall down my cheeks. "I love her. I have to find her."

"Wait! Colin!"

I didn't listen. I took off out the front door and in the direction of the address Billy had sent me. As I was running I texted him to meet me at the diner.

Tatiana had told me before that he had a car, and we were going to need it.

I was a seasoned runner thanks to my athletic career, but it still felt like it took an hour to reach my destination. I ran into the restaurant first, but there was no sign of Tatiana or Val inside. I questioned several waitresses, but they told me that shift change happened not long ago, any waitress who'd been there that morning had already gone home. I rushed back outside, feeling like it was getting harder and harder to catch my breath. I was trying to focus my brain on a next step, but I was so afraid that I couldn't think straight. First my parents, then Tatiana. I couldn't live in a world without them all. I wouldn't.

"Colin!"

I looked over and Billy was rushing in my direction waving his hand through the air. I zeroed in on what was clasped in his hand and my stomach flipped over.

It was Tatiana's phone.

"Where did you find that?" I asked.

"It was down the sidewalk a bit." He handed it over to me and I unlocked it, knowing her passcode was a blend of her parents' birth months and dates.

All of the calls and texts were still unchecked.

"She must have gone missing right after she texted you."

Billy started to cry. "Where is she?"

I pulled my phone out and called Coach Nash again. "Undinger. Did you find Tatiana?" I was a mess and he could hear it. "Shit. Tell me it's not…"

"She's missing," I sniffled. "I don't know where she is. She could be in trouble."

"Well, this is worth getting fired for. I'm sending you Val's address."

A small glimmer of hope sparked out. "You have it?!"

"Yeah, but promise me you won't go yourself. Give this to the police."

I nodded, frantic. "I promise!"

I hung up with Coach Nash and a few seconds later the address rolled in. I looked at Billy. "Would you do anything for Tatiana?"

He nodded and I could see the resolve in his eyes. "Anything. She's not just my best friend. She's the most important person in the world to me."

It must have been hard for him to sit by while she dated Val. "I know the feeling. Let's go. I have Val's address. We have to go and save her."

## 26

## COLIN

I could tell that Billy was hesitant as I shoved my elbow through the window pane on the door to Val's house. He was going along with everything I said, but he was clearly afraid. I felt bad dragging him with me, but he had a car and I didn't. I was afraid if I called the police and Val got wind of it, if Tatiana was still alive, she wouldn't be much longer. The thought made me want to throw up, but I pushed through it the same way I pushed through the shards of glass to reach down and try and unlock Val's door from the inside.

"Are there people watching?" I asked, as I stretched trying to get to the lock, which was just out of reach. I could feel the glass ripping my skin, but I didn't care.

"One lady," Billy replied. "Oh shit. She's coming over."

It didn't change what I was doing. I continued on flicking my fingers at the lock, just grazing over it, but never getting enough of a hold to turn it completely. "Fuck. I can't reach it." I was so erratic that, if there was a better way to do that, it wouldn't have occurred to me. I wanted in. I stood back from the door and started to kick it.

"What are you boys doing?" I heard a woman's voice call out. "I'll call the police."

"Do it!" Billy shouted, even though it was the last thing I wanted. I was already here, and making a fuss, so if he was inside, he knew I was there. I was just praying I could get to Tatiana in time. "The man that lives in this house kidnapped a teenage girl!"

"Oh no," she responded, but seemed to believe us. "Shorter girl, with wavy brown hair?"

Billy and I both whipped around and looked at her. "Do you know her?" She recoiled from me a bit and I tried to calm down. "Did you see her go in here?"

"Not today." She wrapped her robe a little lighter around herself, but she wasn't shielding herself from the cold of the night. "Many times before though."

I went back to kicking the door until it finally burst open from the force. I raced inside yelling at Billy to "Get as much information as you can from the neighbor."

Val lived in a townhome that looked like any pedophile's home. Not in the sense that he had pictures of kids all over the place, but that it looked like it had been selected and decorated to match an ikea catalogue. There was nothing that made it personal, nothing that made it unique. If someone were to try and describe it to someone else, it would sound like they were describing any old home. There were no pictures, no DVDs that might suggest what he was into, not even clothes hanging around. He wanted his place to be bland so that the only thing there was to focus on inside was himself.

I did a sweep of the house. I ran into the kitchen, but it was just as boring in there as it had been in the living room when I first entered, and his bathroom and office had the same mundane qualities. I grabbed his computer, hoping that there might be some evidence inside that a police officer could access, but the thought of waiting for a police officer to find Tatiana made me feel like hope was already lost. I knew how these things went, psychotic people do things all the time simply because they feel like it, just like what had happened with my parents. All it took was a one second snap to ruin people's lives forever.

But my life had already been ruined enough. I'd already lost my parents, I wouldn't lose my world as well.

When I got to the upstairs bedroom, I opened the door, and the sight made me so dizzy I thought I was going to pass out. The bed was affixed with ropes to each of the posts, at the ends of which were clasps for the hands and ankles. Duct tape was on the bedside table, along with a digital camera. A suitcase was open on the bed, and some clothes had already been folded up and packed neatly inside. Whatever was supposed to happen with Tatiana was meant to happen in that bedroom, but in some way she'd interfered with his plans. I didn't know if it was a relief or a nail in the coffin. If they weren't there when the plan was clearly to end up there, then where the hell were they?

"Colin!"

As if to prove to me for definite that there was no one in the house, when Billy's voice screamed out, it echoed across the walls and found me with an additional bass behind it. The townhouse was definitely empty. I made my way back down the stairs that had led me up and exited out onto the front steps. Billy was standing there with the original neighbor who'd approached us, and another, tall man had joined the fray.

"She's not inside?" the male neighbor asked.

"No." I was out of breath from running through the house.

The neighbor put his hands on his hips. "It's a crying shame. I saw that girl going in and out of that house. I knew she was too young to be going there alone. I called the police a couple of times, but whenever they showed up, the girl claimed she was just here for tutoring. I told them it was risky business, but they said that until they have evidence to suggest something's wrong, they can't look into it." He shook his head like a disappointed father. "If it were up to me, I would have cuffed him first and asked questions later."

If only they had. "Please," I begged. "Do you know anything else that could help us? Do you know where he might have taken her?"

Both neighbor's heads turned to the sky as they thought on it. Finally, the woman clapped her hands and went running towards her house across the street. We could see as she stood in the doorway sifting through something near the door. Finally, she pulled a piece of paper, holding it triumphantly above her head, and then came running back.

She handed the paper to me with shaking

hands. "I forgot! Last year he told me that his mother died. He decided not to sell her house and I know he spent some time there after her passing. He got in touch with me after being there a couple of weeks to say he was staying longer and asked me to forward his mail."

It was like gold in my hands until I read the address. "Colorado Springs." The words whispered out of me and Billy drew closer to me and looked over the address with his own eyes.

"Fuck. That's like five hours from here." Billy looked up at the neighbors, and I could hear his voice like the distant hum of an air conditioner. Much louder was the blood coursing through my ears, beating against my head with fear that we were already too late. "Colin?"

A gentle shake knocked me just loose enough to focus. "Yeah?"

"I said we have to call the Colorado Springs police, right?"

The same fear that gripped me an hour before took hold again. The neighbor's retelling of the police continuously not caring about Tatiana's well being spun into the thought of Val thinking that the police were coming to take Tatiana away forever; he'd kill them both for sure.

"We can't."

Billy stepped away from me and looked at me like I'd lost my mind. "What?"

"We can't call the police. Val was willing to do all of this because he didn't want to let her go. He'd packed his bags in there, he was already prepared to do something irreversible." As I spoke, the female neighbor brought her hands to her mouth. "If we call the police, he could flip out and kill her and then maybe even himself." I didn't like saying the words out loud, like they cemented them into the fabric of reality. "We have to go."

"No." The male neighbor waved his hands. "I'm not putting up with this anymore. You're kids. The police need to step up and do their fucking jobs."

I wasn't sure when I'd started crying, but I was. I wished more than anything that my parents weren't gone. If they were still with me, they'd know what to do. "Please," I begged, my voice barely audible. "Please don't call them. I don't… I can't…" My chest was so tight I expected my ability to breathe to cease any moment. "We'll go, so please…"

The neighbors stared at me with the same conflicted eyes Coach Nash had stared at me through back when I first told him about Val and Tatiana. I knew what I was asking them. I was asking them to go against their better judgements as adults. To trust in the hands of children what men and women trained in whole academies to take care of. None of that mattered to me. I just needed to get to Tatiana.

"Come on, Billy. We have to go." I gave the neighbors one final, painful look, hoping it would sell my case for me because I was out of both carrots and sticks. "If you call them, she'll die. I hope you can live with that." Billy followed me without hesitation, which I was pleased for, but even as he climbed into the driver's seat, I could see his hands shaking. I grabbed his arm and pulled him back out. "You navigate. I'll drive."

## 27

## TATIANA

My head hurt. It felt like I'd chosen to settle it against some sharp rock that was continuously stabbing into the spot where I'd been struck. My eyes remained closed, probably for the fact that I was afraid of what I'd find when I opened them. The stale, unknown stench of a place I didn't recognize floated around me, blended with the faint and distant smell of a cologne I knew that Val wore. I shifted my body to one side, and the feeling of a bed beneath me might have been comforting if I hadn't simultaneously realized my arms and legs were restricted from movement. My eyes flew open, taking in the foreign bedroom around me. My gaze went up to where my wrists were bound to the posts of an extravagant, though extremely outdated bed frame. It followed the twisting of a rose and vine pattern on the musty bedspread down to where my ankles had met a similar fate. I was stuck.

"Help!" I fought against my restraints, hoping to break myself free. "Help me! Help!" The rope that had been used to tie me was a thickly bound cord, made for the purpose of keeping someone from accomplishing exactly what I was attempting to. "Someone, please! Help me!"

My voice was throwing into hysterics, and as I flailed I caught a glimpse of the sky through the slit in the window's curtains; it was night, and not new night, but a deep blue. How long had I been gone? How stupid was I letting Billy know I was safe before I got home? Why would I turn my back to Val when I had been smart enough up to that point to protect myself? Why had I allowed arrogance and fear to control my actions and lie to me that Val wouldn't hurt me, he was just hurting? Colin's calm face, still sleeping in my bed spoke across my brain and tears started to roll down my eyes.

At least I got to see him one last time. At least he knew that I loved him.

I said a silent apology to my parents. They trusted me to be responsible. They'd always tried to be open with me and ask that I do the same. How did I repay them for how wonderful they'd been to me? By dating a psycho and getting myself kidnapped and probably killed.

I rattled the bed again. "Help me!" The door to the bedroom flew open and Val came rushing inside. The sight of him filled me with dread and started to shake my head and make every attempt to back away even though I knew I would fail. "No! Get away from me! Help!"

Val dropped to the bed, using a knee to prop himself up, and threw his hands over my mouth. "Shh, shh. It's okay. It's okay, baby. Shh." I was whimpering under his hands, part of me wishing he would just skip to the final step and spare me anymore torture. He started to stroke my hair softly. "It's okay, my love. You're safe. I know it's a little scary being tied up, but I just didn't want to lose you." He was speaking with a warm, soft voice as if it was going to convince me that he was just doing what any rational, caring lover would do. "I didn't want to do this to you, you know? I tried to warn you. I love you and want you to be only mine forever. I love you more than anyone ever will. You know that. You've seen it. I'm the only one you can be with."

Behind his rationalizing tone was something manic. He was half trying to convince himself. I tried kissing the palm of his hand. I only had a couple of options. Continue to struggle and fight and probably end up dead in a ditch somewhere, or sweet talk him and hope for some grace. If I could get him to believe that I loved him and was sorry, maybe he'd untie me. Then it would just be about waiting for an opportunity, and of course hoping I wasn't in some cliche cabin in the woods, though his not wanting me to scream was evidence enough that I wasn't.

I kissed his hand again, trying my hardest to soften my eyes. Finally, he pulled his hand back with a gentle smile. "You don't only have to kiss my hand you know."

"Then kiss my lips," I replied.

He obliged, dipping into me and setting his mouth on mine. He pulled away and grinned down at me. "You know, right? That I'm the one who loves you most?"

I nodded. "I know. I didn't want to break up with you. Once everyone found out, I was afraid. Afraid to lose you."

Val's eyes drifted closed as he considered my words. He nodded and I gained some confidence that he was accepting them. "I should have known. You push the things away that you're afraid of."

I didn't like him speaking words about me that

had some validity to them. I'd cost Colin and I five years and turned myself into a kidnap victim because of it. "I know. I just thought, if we were going to have to end, I wanted to do it to save myself the pain."

Val's eyes, full of hypnotic love, danced over me. "I will never leave you as long as you'll have me." He reached down and cupped his hand over the side of my neck, and the second I felt the miniscule unsettling of the necklace I wore there, I knew I'd fucked myself. Val's pinky hooked the chain and pulled it free of where I'd tucked it into my sweater. "What's this?"

I had no lies to tell. I'd maintained the entire scope of our relationship that I hated football, it made me think of Colin. I watched his expression shift as he studied the half a football locket and when his eyes came to mine again, they were no longer full of love, but of fury.

"You're lying."

"No." I shook my head. "My parents--"

"You're lying!" His voice bellowed out in a loud scream. "Did Colin give this to you?" He snatched it from around my neck and it felt like he took Colin with it, like he'd snatched the very skin off my body. His hand took my face into it like the forceful claw of a crab. The force of his fingers were pure pain against my jaw. "You're mine," he growled. "You will be mine, or you will be no ones."

I started to cry again. "Please." The small strand of Val that I felt like I could reason with had left the building leaving only this monster behind. "Help!" I screamed. "Help me!"

Val reached for something out of sight, but when his hand came back into view, it was a fresh roll of silver duct tape. He unraveled a layer of it, which he ripped off with his teeth like a bear biting into the flesh of a fish, then he slapped it over my mouth and pressed it down so hard it felt like my bones were going to crack. I did my best to scream against the tape, but it was no use, my voice wasn't louder than a muffle.

"It's going to be okay, beautiful." He kissed the part of the duct tape that covered my lips. "You need some time to get around it. Maybe you're just hungry." One doesn't eat and suddenly become comfortable with kidnap. "I'll go get you some food."

Val walked out of the room, leaving the door open behind him. I tried pulling at the cords binding me, but it was no use, they weren't going to give. I could see the objects around the room, taunting me with how trapped I was. The window I could easily climb through, the small, floral table lamp that would probably work well to smash over Val's head. Everything I saw gave me an idea for defending myself and escaping, if only I could get free, which I couldn't.

The fight to survive left me bit by bit until there was nothing left. I had backed myself into a very dark, very lonely corner. I left my mind to travel to sweeter places, at least it could escape where I couldn't. I imagined how lovely the Bahamas might be over the summer. Colin topless in swim trunks, splashing with me through the ocean water. Trying to find some way to sleep in the same room without my parents' knowledge. Putting the worries of school, and Val, and Colin leaving for college out of our mind and just focus on being together. That would have been nice. Would they still go without me? They'd probably be too sad. It was still several months away, maybe they would go in my honor?

Val re-entered the room after what felt like hours, carrying a plate with a steak and potatoes on it. Only the best for his victims, I supposed? "Sorry that took so long, Tati. I wanted to make you something good, but my mom only had health nut food around."

Mom? Were we at his mom's house? Where was she? Was she allowing her son to keep a teenage woman captive against her will? I looked at the bed again. No. I was in her bed. Was she dead? Did he kill her so he could turn her home into a cage for me? I tried not to focus on the idea.

He sat on the edge of the bed and set the plate on the table next to me. The smells wafted into my nose and reminded me that I hadn't had anything to eat all day. Val laughed at what must have been a tell that I was hungry and ready to eat.

"Okay, okay. Just give me a second to take my jacket off and then I'll take the tape off, but you're not going to scream are you?" I shook my head, now starving and staring at the food. He rubbed my head. "Good girl."

He stood up and turned towards the closet to unzip his jacket and tossed it inside, but when he turned to face me again, his eyes landed on me as dark, hungry irises, and not for food. The sound that gurgled out of him was unfamiliar, like the hunting call of a predator when it zeroed in on its prey.

"I've never told you, but I have a thing for tying women up. I thought you were still too young yet, but I was planning to introduce you eventually." I didn't like the intentions behind his voice. "I should have known that seeing you tied up would do something to me eventually." He grabbed the base of his shirt and lifted it over his head and I felt like I was going to puke up the lack of sustenance in my body. "I know you're hungry, but please just wait a little bit longer."

He walked across the bedroom back towards the bed and straddled himself over me. What little struggle was left in me came out, twisting my face to keep it from his and pulling at the ropes even though I knew they wouldn't budge. Val kissed along my neck and over my jaw until he was up to my mouth. He peeled the duct tape back with a crawling sting and forced his lips against mine, pushing his tongue inside without permission. Leeches could have been sucking blood from me and not made me feel so lifeless. I didn't want this. I didn't want him. One of his hands broke loose and smoothed it's way down my torso, over my breasts, across my stomach, and started to climb beneath the hem of my jeans.

I shook my head, tears streaming down my face, and Val lifted his head. "It's okay, baby. I love you. It's okay."

"No," I whined. "I don't want to."

"You'll love it soon."

I was about to fade to black. To untie my soul from the dock of my body and let it drift out to open sea lest it find some more beautiful place to float to. I closed my eyes and pulled my attention away from Val's hands journeying lower, until I jumped at the sound of a crash from somewhere outside the bedroom. Val stopped short. He looked over his shoulder, not speaking, barely breathing. He turned his attention back to me and resumed his movements until another crash, this time louder, rocked out.

Val climbed off of me and I felt like I'd been saved by a mystery angel. Even if the crash was the result of a burglar coming in to kill us both, I'd be happy for that.

"HELP!"

It was a risk, but it was worth it. If it wasn't a burglar, or even if it was, if I could alert them to my distress, it may save my life. Val reached back down over me and returned the duct tape to it's spot over my mouth before I could get another word out. He walked out of the bedroom and then there was nothing but eerie silence. I listened for anything. The sound of Val walking, the sound of another crash, the sound of anything that might indicate what was happening, but nothing found me. Was it just seconds passing me by? Minutes? Hours? I wasn't wishing for Val to return, but not knowing was riddling my body with anxiety.

And then a yell, loud, piercing. It was definitely

inside the house. It led to a cacophony of grunts and groans as it sounded like two people tussling around. There were bangs and bumps as the two people no doubt bumped into things, and different crashes suggested the knocking over of items made of glass. There was clearly a fight going on. I glanced at the window, but saw no lights that would indicate the police had arrived. Maybe it *was* just a petty thief.

In the next second, a familiar head of hair crossed the threshold and I was convinced I was dreaming. The fighting hadn't ceased, but somehow, Billy was running into the room, the front of his head drenched in sweat. He raced over to me and pulled the duct tape off, yelping in response to my screech of pain.

"Billy?" I started to cry. "What? How?"

Billy was already working to free me from the ropes. "I'll explain later. Colin's in trouble!"

It took him a minute to get me loose, but eventually he did. The only thing on my mind was getting to Colin. If he was fighting with Val, there was no telling what would happen. I could say with absolute certainty that they would kill one another over me, and the very last thing I wanted was a murder charge on Colin's hands. I made for the noises of struggle, screaming at Billy to call the police.

He grabbed my arm and pulled me back. "You should go. I'll help Colin."

Billy was pale as a ghost and looked like he was ready to pass out. "No offense, but you look like you're on death's door yourself. Call the police. Call my parents and tell them I'm safe."

Billy didn't argue. He turned and headed off, obviously knowing his way through the house more than I did, and I continued on, walking in the direction of the fight. I cleared a long hallway and saw Colin and Val struggling amidst the antique appointed living room. Several objects were already shattered on the ground, and to my horror, Val was waving a black pistol through the air with Colin fighting to keep it away from him. I didn't think twice. I bolted into the room and leapt up onto Val's back.

"Tatiana! Get out of here!" Colin shouted.

"Not without you!" I clung to Val's back as best I could, identifying an unbroken lamp on an end table. "Back up!" It was just out of reach, but if Colin could push us back far enough, I could get to it.

Colin did his best to push, but it turned out to be a fatal error. Val managed to work his arm between himself and Colin, and when the ear split-ting sound of a gunshot rang out, I screamed, "Colin!"

Colin buckled, but like a defensive lineman trying to stop a sack, he dug his feet in and forced Val back. As I reached the lamp, I grabbed it and smashed it over Val's head. All three of us went dropping to the floor and the gun went scattering across the carpet. I was able to get to my feet - unlike Val who was groaning and rubbing his head, and Colin who was taking in sharp, short breaths and holding his stomach. I rushed over to the gun, picked it up, and cocked it, aiming it at Val.

Val looked at me with defeat in his eyes and settled against the floor, accepting his fate, but I had no intention of killing him. I wasn't going to let him take any more of my life than he already had. Being careful to keep the gun pointed against Val, I knelt next to Colin. Tears cascaded down my cheeks as I imagined losing him. I put my free hand on the wound and pressed, causing Colin to scream out.

"Just hang in there. Help is coming."

## 28

# TATIANA

## Three Months Later...

"It sounds like your new permanent teacher will be Mrs. Jay Stammler." My father peeled down the paper he was looking at. "And I sincerely hope you will keep your hands to yourself."

I supposed I had earned myself the trouble I was in. My parents opted not to punish me in the wake of everything that happened with Val, but I was far from out of the woods. I'd been getting comments like those for the past few months. Really, any time I got too close to anyone even remotely adult age, my parents started to treat me like a dog who'd just caught sight of a cat across the street. They must have assumed that would be far worse than any traditional punishment they could muster up, and they were right, especially with my dad's inability to say anything quietly, middle of the grocery store be damned.

"Dad, I'm not going to do anything. Val tricked me, and besides, I'm with Colin now." I spooned at the cereal in front of me, looking over at the empty barstool at my side.

"Well, I would have assumed you'd be doing your school work, only for me to find out you were doing something else."

"Dad!" I glared at him. Absolutely having my parents discuss my sexual history was worse than having my phone taken away or getting grounded.

A creak alerted me to movement on the stairs. I jumped up from my spot and ran over to the stairs, just in time to catch Colin hobbling his way down with my mom braced behind him. I held out a hand, but Colin ignored it.

"I've got it, gorgeous," he grumbled.

I rolled my eyes. "That's what you said yesterday and then you *fell down half the flight of stairs.*"

"I wanted to do that." He pecked me on my nose as he limped by me.

My mom patted the back of his head. "Of course you did, dear."

The gunshot that Colin had received at Val's hand had been bad, but fortunately not fatal. He was recovering, though slowly, even slower than he would be if he hadn't kept demanding he was fine and doing things that exacerbated his injury.

"Morning, Colin," my dad greeted as Colin finally made it into the kitchen.

My mom guided him down onto his regular barstool and then walked over to our eating nook where her laptop was sitting and picked it up. "Big news this morning."

"Morning," Colin replied, a little delayed, a flat irritation to his voice.

I returned to my seat next to him. "What's wrong?"

"The doctor didn't clear me to play football again. The season's half over!"

I scoffed. "Sweetie, you took a bullet to the stomach, not a ball to the face."

"And if you'd just settle down and let it heal, you'd recover quicker," my mom threw in quickly.

"And if you'd listen to them, they wouldn't be nagging at you at," my dad checked his watch, "8:30 in the morning on a Saturday."

Colin chuckled and my mom held up her hands in surrender. "Point taken."

I leaned over and kissed Colin on his cheek. "Sorry."

He rubbed his nose against mine. "It's okay."

My dad cleared his throat and I backed away from Colin and stuck out my tongue at my dad and he stuck his back out at me. "Behave yourself. WHICH IS WHAT I EXPECTED FROM YOUR EDUCA--"

"Okay dad!" Colin started laughing and I dropped my jaw. "Stop, you're making it worse!"

"It should be worse," my mom sang. "Thank you for participating, Colin."

Colin nodded with pride. "Of course. This is fun."

My mom opened her laptop and after tapping away at the keyboard a little bit, she turned the screen to face us, pressed play on a video, and then walked around to stand next to my dad.

A news video started to play that showed Val being walked out of a courthouse in handcuffs. There were crowds of people on both sides screaming at him as he was loaded into a squad car. "The town of Orchard Mesa can sleep a little easier today as former high school science teacher,

Val Kepler, is found guilty of all the charges brought against him by the district attorney. The town has been the source of misfortune recently, as a burglary gone wrong resulted in the deaths of Ryan and Helena Undinger." Simultaneously, my mom and I put our hands on Colin, hers on his back and mine on his arm. "Their son, Colin Undinger would go on to heroically save his girlfriend, Tatiana Marquette, after she was kidnapped by the teacher she was involved in an illicit, sexual relationship with Val Kepler. Kepler was sentenced to 109 years in prison today, with no possibility of parole. His charges included attempted rape, statutory rape, attempted murder, assault with a deadly weapon, child endangerment, and kidnapping. The judge who oversaw the case, an Orchard Mesa native, had this to say:"

"I was shocked and appalled by the actions of this individual. Remaining impartial was difficult. I wanted to sentence him to a thousand years on the spot, but the evidence was insurmountable, and the jury came to the right decision today." The judge, an elderly man with a bald head, and a liver-spot stained face, looked directly into the camera. "And the bravery of young Colin Undinger, who only lost his parents a month prior, to race into danger, that's a man Orchard Mesa can be proud of. Can't wait to see you back on the field, young man. Go Tigers!"

I rubbed Colin's hand, and that time when I kissed him on his cheek, my parents remained silent.

My mom looked at her watch and yelped. "Oh. We gotta go kids, we're late."

Colin was finally eighteen, and my mom had put off his parents' lawyer for a while after everything happened with me and Val. He had some decisions to make about everything his parents had left him, but unlike the fearful, uncertain way he approached the subject a few months ago, he walked into the lawyer's office now with his head held high. He sat down in the leather chair and folded his hands on top of the desk like a proper businessman. I was proud of him, but he also looked sexy in his navy blue suit with his hair slicked back and falling down his neck. I'd be glad when he had fully healed, not just because I didn't want him to be suffering anymore, but because his injury had effectively brought our barely-started sex life to a screeching halt.

"I gotta say, I was shocked to hear that you picked a college so close," the lawyer began. "Your parents had been saving for quite some time, expecting you to pick a place further away."

Colin had been offered full-ride scholarships from several major colleges, including eight of the previous years' Big Ten. He hadn't played since he had been shot, but his recent notoriety in the news caused people to look him up and some of his football reels went viral.

Colin glanced over at me, sitting on the couch against the wall as my mom took the other chair. "Yeah. My whole world is here, so…"

The lawyer smiled. "Well, I'm glad to see you doing so much better. I realize this is arduous. It's never fun for a kid to have to take care of these types of affairs. So, let's start with--"

"I'm turning over the deed of the house to my aunt. She's going to maintain it, probably rent it out, until I'm ready to move back into it or sell it. Any money from renting it out will be put into a savings account that she has emergency access to, but otherwise will be used solely to pay the mortgage and other expenses. I've already asked the bank to transfer some starting funds to that account to handle the house's costs until it's ready to be rented."

My mom, myself, and the lawyer's jaws all

dropped. He sounded so confident, so official. "W-well, excellent," the lawyer replied. "And--"

"Sorry to keep cutting you off," Colin continued. "I'll be taking over Undinger's after I graduate college. Until then, Harriet," Undinger's long-time manager, "will oversee the business. She'll still run any major decisions by me, but honestly, I trust her more with the restaurant at this point, so I've given her complete control over the restaurant. Even when I take over full time, my hope is to be mostly hands off. Harriet's much more prepared than I am."

My mom smiled broadly. "He's been working hard to put it all together."

The lawyer laughed. "I see. I guess that just leaves the matter of where you'll live."

"I'm going to pick up the keys to an apartment on Clairmont and 8th after this meeting." Colin's confident smile grew large on his face. "I'll be there for the foreseeable future. I used some of the money my parents left me to pay rent a year in advance so I just focus on school and those expenses."

The lawyer folded her hands, impressed. "It seems like you've got everything in order." She looked over at me. "You've got yourself a good one, girl." She winked.

I nodded. "Trust me, I know."

The apartment Colin had mentioned, was one we picked out together. My parents tried desperately to get him to stay, but now that he was recovering from losing his parents, he was getting to the point that asking for so much was draining him. He promised to visit frequently, and my mom made him agree to Sunday dinners. In truth, Colin probably would have been happy to continue staying with us, but my parents were too solicitous of him, and I think it made him miss his own parents. He hadn't said as much, but part of the reason he was moving into his own place was so that he could officially distance himself from things that reminded him of their untimely passing. Being at our place, especially that it had us under the same roof, was a reminder of his circumstances, even if it led to other ones that made him happy.

Less important, though still worth mentioning, was the fact that my dad had behaved exactly as I predicted when we finally told them we were together. If Colin's door even blew in the wind, my dad was next to him half a second later, grilling him on where he was going. It wasn't like we could do anything, even if we wanted to, and the structure finally toppled when my dad actually dropped to the ground and checked under the table in the dining room when we were eating dinner one night. Apparently we'd been smiling too much and he thought we were playing footsie.

We were, but that didn't make his behavior any less horrifying.

That night, Colin and I facetimed from our separate bedrooms to look at apartments together and picked the one we were now standing in the middle of. Colin signed the lease and got the keys and now we were seeing it for the first time. He kept calling it 'our new home' and it gave me fuzzy feelings every time we did so.

My mom fluttered around the place like a typical mom, checking all the faucets, outlets, and floorboards for signs of imperfections. She was yelling instructions at Colin from every corner of the apartment about how to keep different types of wood clean, hacks when washing clothes, and the best way to arrange his bedroom. We just let her do what she was going to do while we just stood in the empty living room hand-in-hand. I couldn't wait to decorate.

"I'm surprised you picked this one," Colin started finally. "It's kind of small."

I set my head against his shoulder. "It was the closest one. Besides, it's perfect because you'll be here."

He kissed my forehead. "I hate that we have to wait so long for you to live here too."

"Oh, I've got a plan for that," I replied.

"Colin! The handle on the toilet is loose! We have to get you a new handle!"

I rolled my eyes and Colin shook his head. "Okay, ma! We can go get one when we leave."

She popped her head out from the hallway. "Oh, good idea. Let's just start gathering the things you're going to need. You need a toilet bowl brush, curtains for the bedroom, and it's cheaper to buy toilet paper in bulk. Oh! I'll make a list."

She disappeared again and I laughed. "Ha, joke's on you. They're going to be *more* annoying now."

Colin just shook the idea away. "So, you were saying, a plan?"

"Oh yeah, I'm just going to start bringing my stuff over little by little. I'll spend a day here, then two, then three, until I'm here all the time." I kissed him quickly. "I'll be moved in by Christmas."

Colin smiled down at me. "Let's hope so." Absent-mindedly, my hands went to the spot where my locket used to hang around my neck. It wasn't there anymore. The police had recovered it in the investigation into Val, but it became evidence, and I probably wouldn't ever see it again. "You miss it."

I realized what Colin was referring to and dropped my hand. "Yeah. I feel like I'd just gotten it back and now it's gone again."

Colin reached into his pocket and pulled out a medium-sized rectangular box. He tipped back the cover, revealing a sterling silver chain that flooded down into a couple of diamonds that surrounded the word 'soon.'

"I wanted to be the one who bought it this time." I was speechless. He pulled it from the box and hung it around my neck, kissing me on my cheek before wrapping his arms around my waist and pulling me back against him. He set his mouth near my ear. "Consider it a promise."

I maneuvered until I was facing Colin and took him into a full kiss, hoping he could feel all of my emotions carrying across it. "I love you."

"And I you," Colin replied. "Forever."

---

Thanks for reading THE ENEMY NEXT DOOR. Don't Miss SWORN ENEMIES, the next standalone book in THE FOOTBALL BOYS series. And if you loved this story, consider leaving a review on Amazon. **It would be amazing!**

**Get an alert when I release a new book:**

SMS: Text REBEL to 77948 (US only)

EMAILs: join at www.RebelHart.net

## WANT TO BE A REBEL?

Join my Group of Rebels to chat with me and other fans. I'd love to have you there!

# ABOUT THE AUTHOR

Rebel Hart is an author of Contemporary and Dark Romance novels. All her books are available in the Kindle Unlimited program on Amazon at: author.to/RebelHart

**NEVER MISS A NEW RELEASE:**
Follow Rebel on Amazon
Follow Rebel on Bookbub

Text REBEL to 77948 to don't miss any of her books (US only) or sign up at www.RebelHart.net to get an email alert when her next book is out.

authorrebelhart@gmail.com

CONNECT WITH REBEL HART:

## ALSO BY REBEL HART

For a full list of my books go to:

www.RebelHart.net

Printed in Great Britain
by Amazon

43256830R00182